I0659844

SHADY DEALS

THE UNBRIDLED SERIES

by

CINDY MCDONALD

Shady Deals
The UnBridled Series

All Rights Reserved © 2013 by Cindy McDonald

No part of this book may be reproduced or transmitted in any form or by any means, graphic, electronic, or mechanical, including photocopying, recording, taping, or by any information storage retrieval system without the written permission of the author.

For information call: 304-995-1295
or Email: cindys.mcdonald@gmail.com

This book is a work of fiction. Names, characters, places, and incidents are products of the author's imagination or are used fictitiously. Any resemblance to actual events or locales or persons, living or dead, is entirely coincidental.

Designed by Acorn Book Services

Publication Managed by Acorn Book Services
www.acornbookservices.com
acornbookservices@gmail.com
304-995-1295

Cover designed by Todd Aune
Spokane, Washington
www.projetoonline.com

ISBN -10: 0991368002
ISBN-13: 978-0-9913680-0-6

Printed in the United States of America

ACKNOWLEDGEMENTS

There are many people I wish to thank who had a hand in the publishing and pre-publishing process of Shady Deals. My dear friend and confidant, Linda Taylor, who always reads my manuscripts before they go to my editor—thank you for all of those wonderful "suggestions" of yours—I don't know what I'd do without them! I wish to thank my wonderful publishing manager, good friend, and fellow author, Lauren Carr, for her constant support and insightful editing; and the creative genius behind this fabulous cover, Todd Aune. Thank you to those at Acorn Book Services that worked behind-the-scenes on my behalf. Last but certainly never least, I want to thank my husband, Saint Bill, your love and support always takes my breath away.

Thank you.

TABLE OF CONTENTS

SHADY DEALS

THE UNBRIDLED SERIES

We tell lies when we are afraid...afraid of what we don't know, afraid of what others will think, afraid of what will be found out about us. But every time we tell a lie, the thing that we fear grows stronger.

Tad Williams

With lies you may get ahead in the world—but you can never go back.

Russian Proverb

~ PROLOGUE ~

"Take off your clothes," Dr. Holden Reese closed the door to his veterinarian office at Keystone Downs Thoroughbred Racetrack. His hot gaze slid over Kate West's slender curves. He dropped the deadbolt into the locked position.

A shiver skittering down her spine, Kate turned to him. She wore a red tank top and a pair of tight Levi jeans. Her long blonde tresses were pulled back into a ponytail. The florescent lighting glinted off the silver hoop earrings that dangled from her earlobes.

While her full lips parted, her eyebrows rose. "Ever heard of sexual harassment, Dr. Reese?" Unbuckling his belt, he strode toward her. He took the vet box from her hand to set it on a nearby shelving unit and then pushed her against the block wall.

Holden was a six foot two solidly muscled male. His deep brown eyes burned into her baby blues.

Caging her between his arms, Holden reached behind her head to pull out her hair band to let it spill like a golden waterfall about her shoulders. Fisting his fingers through the locks, he tilted her head back to hold her in place. "Oh, I've heard of it, Miss West, and I have every intention of taking you on my desk." He nipped at her earlobe before making his way slowly down her neck. "Do you want to scream?"

Kate's fingers splayed wide on the wall that she was pinned against. Everything female in her clenched at his teasing nips and licks and the way he smoothed his lips over her heating skin. She could feel her nipples pushing to stiff peaks against the inside of her bra. She swallowed hard and let go of a groan from deep in her throat. She rasped, "Do you want me to scream, Dr. Reese?"

Holden smiled against her shoulder. He whispered, "When I make you come."

He pressed his lips to hers. Pushing his tongue into her mouth, he savored her taste. Possessing her, he tangled his fingers tighter through her hair.

Kate wrapped her arms around his waist and pushed up on her toes to capture more from the kiss when Holden let go of her hair and grabbed her by the shoulders. Astonished that the kiss had ended so abruptly, she blinked back.

"You were stripping..." He stepped back to take in the show about to start.

Biting her lip, Kate planted her hands on her hips.

His gaze never wavered while he unbuttoned his jeans. Urging her, he said, "The desk is waiting, my pretty little assistant."

"And if I refuse? Will you fire me?"

He lowered his zipper with slow unerring precision. "You won't refuse." He whipped his T-shirt over his head to bare his sculpted biceps and abs. Sporting a sinful come-on look that should've been in the category of a felony, he tossed his shirt to the floor.

"That's not fair!" Kate blurted.

His mouth curved into a wicked smile. "I'll use whatever weapons at my disposal to get you naked. I've been fantasizing since yesterday about doing it on my desk with my sexy little employee."

Glancing at the desk, Kate noted that it had been cleared for the event.

Holden added, "You won't mention this to your boyfriend, will you?"

Kate rolled her eyes at his suggested role-play. Quirky. What fun. She went along. "He's the jealous type, you know. Not to mention that he could probably beat the snot out of you."

"I'll take my chances." Holden rolled his right index finger in the air at her. "Let the stripping commence."

Knowing that he rather enjoyed a demure display, Kate peeked at him through her lashes. She slowly slipped her tank over her head. Tossing it to the floor, she left him to ogling her dainty blue lace bra. She unbuttoned her jeans, lowered the zipper bit by bit, and then she shimmied her hips until they slipped down her legs to pool at her feet. Swiftly she kicked them aside. She stood before him in a tiny lace thong and the lace bra.

He licked his lips.

She was driving him crazy. Through the open fly of his jeans, she could see the column of his erection bulging from his boxer brief. She liked it. Her lips curled at his delicious anticipation.

Slowly, she reached back to unhook the bra. Rather than allowing it to fall to the floor, she cupped her breasts in her palms to hold the bra in place.

Holden sucked in a deep breath while he watched her bite her lower lip as she kneaded her breasts in a circular motion, until she slowly let the bra slip down her arms to fall at her feet.

Holden grabbed her hands and restrained them behind her back before she could hook her thumbs through the bands of the thong. Sealing his mouth over hers, he kissed her hard while pulling her against his arousal.

"Leave a little for me," he snarled. He released her hands to grab her buttocks and lift her until she wrapped her legs around his waist. Lips locked, he carried her to the desk and set her down gently. He murmured, "I don't want to hurry my fantasy. I want to savor it, baby."

Pulling away from the kiss, she whispered, "I don't know, my boyfriend will be coming to pick me up soon for the bonfire party at our farm tonight. He doesn't like it when I'm late."

Holden's eyes brightened. "I almost forgot about that." He brushed a lock of hair from her cheek with the pad of his thumb. His eyes narrowed when he asked, "Is the whole party taking place outside?"

Confused by the question, Kate cocked her head while considering the position they were presently in. "Yes..."

"No one will be in the barn?"

"No..."

Carefully, he laid her across the desk to admire her dusty pink nipples standing at attention while waiting for him to nip. Thoughtfully, he ran his fingers along the inside of the elastic band that secured her thong. Kate's tummy tightened at the sultry tickle. The sinful grin returned to his handsome face. "Mmmm, another fantasy just came to mind, Miss West. The rugged cowboy breezes into town and seduces the sassy cowgirl in the hayloft. At first she isn't willing, but soon she succumbs to his cowboy charms."

Shaking her head, Kate chuckled, "Please, one fantasy at a time or I won't be able to keep up, cowboy."

She was right.

He decided to fulfill this fantasy right now. There would be plenty of time this evening for the other—if he could get her alone in the loft. Thinking of a clever way to lure her into the barn loft of her father's Thoroughbred farm, Westwood, he smiled.

Dropping both of his hands on either side of her, he lowered his face to kiss her between her breasts, when the cell phone in his hip pocket began to ring and vibrate. He groaned.

Kate giggled. "That's a mood killer."

"Not for me." He ran his tongue over her stiff nipple.

"Aren't you going to answer it?"

"No."

"Holden, someone could need the vet. You should at least look at the number."

"Really?"

"Really."

"See, I knew there was a good reason that I proposed to you. You keep me on track. By the way, have you told the family about our engagement?"

"Answer the phone, Holden."

He let out a frustrated sigh as he yanked the phone from his pocket to look at the screen: Chip

Walker. Shit. Reaching across her body, he grabbed the handle to the middle drawer of the desk, pulled it open, flipped the phone in, and then slammed the drawer shut.

"It's nobody important enough to interrupt this moment." He looked into her crystal blue eyes full of desire. Raking his fingers through her hair, he said, "Nothing is more important than you are." His fingers slipped from her hair and down her neck until he cupped her breast in his hand. "Now where was I?"

* * * * *

Chip Walker thumbed the END button on his cell phone hard. Doc Reese hadn't answered his calls or his texts in three days. Reese was getting too independent. He wasn't respecting his authority. Reese could blow his whole operation to smithereens. The operation had been compromised six months ago, but he had managed to dodge that bullet. He couldn't afford another mishap. Reese needed to conform. Reese needed to fall in line. Immediately.

CINDY MCDONALD

~ PART ONE ~

SHADES OF GRAY

~ ONE ~

Whew! It had been a long, draining day. It seemed that all the horses at Keystone Downs Racetrack were haunted by some ailment or another today. They were high as a kite or sick as a dog. The horses were irritable and kicky, which made Doctor Ben Spears feel every moment of his sixty-two years.

Glad that the day had come to an end and that his assistant, Ava West, was on her way home, Doc Spears plunked down into his chair behind his desk in his vet office, nestled amongst the stable, on the backside of Keystone Downs. The walls were made of blocks and the floor was cement. Tending to be cold in the winter and damp in the summer, the dingy office suited him just fine.

Doc Spears had been a Pennsylvania state veterinarian for over thirty years. The people of the Thoroughbred racetrack were his family, and the horses were like his children.

Thinking he may be able to catch a few z's, he dragged his fingers through his pure white hair and then leaned his head back against the chair. He closed his eyes when a stiff knock at the door interrupted his solace.

Cursing under his breath, he straightened in the chair, rubbed his eyes, and called out, "Come on in."

Two men hurried through the door.

Jockey agent Tom Jacobs stuck his head out the door and looked up and down the shed row before swiftly closing it behind him. Mopping his receded hairline with a rag, the short middle-aged man leaned against the wall. The bald part of his head gleamed with sweat from under the thin combover. He wore gold chains around his neck and a turquoise ring on his fat pinky finger. He usually had a smooth demeanor and an even smoother Southern drawl, but he was less than cool and collected under his present circumstances.

The corner of Doc's mouth kicked up in amusement as he laced his fingers behind his head and leaned further back in his chair. "What's the matter, Tom? Too old for this shit?"

Tossing him a baleful look, Tom crossed his arms over his chest. "I'm not too thrilled to be involved in your shit at all, Doc. If I didn't owe the federal government a generous sum of tax dollars, I wouldn't be. Now, can we just get on with it?"

Doc sized up the young man who had accompanied Tom into his office.

He was about five foot three inches, maybe four. Slightly built, he came in at approximately one hundred and ten pounds and appeared to be all of thirteen years old.

Doc knew that was only his age and eyesight playing tricks on him. There was no way they were going to send a thirteen-year-old boy to handle a situation like this.

The young man busied himself taking in the contents of the shelving units along the far wall of Doc's office. They were stacked with bottles of equine medicines, boxes of latex gloves, hoses, boxes of syringes, and jars of antiseptic gels. He then took a look at the desk, which was covered with bottles of equine medicines, latex gloves, hoses, syringes, and several jars of antiseptic gels holding down a hotchpotch of paperwork.

Finally, his eyes met Doc's. "I assume you're Dr. Benjamin Spears, my contact. Mr. Jacobs is my agent."

The veterinarian pushed to his feet and extended his hand. "Call me Doc, most everyone around here does, and your name is…"

"Dave Blake…" The young man's handshake was good and firm. Doc liked that.

A firm knock sounded on the door.

Tom Jacob's eyes grew wide and his face flushed.

Rolling his eyes at the nervous Nellie, Doc called out, "Come in."

The door pushed open. Shane West stepped inside and was rather taken aback by all the company that Doc had in his office. "Did I catch you at a bad time, Doc?"

"Not at all. Shane, this is Dave Blake. He's a new bug boy under Tom's agency. Isn't that right, Tom?" Doc raised an eyebrow in Tom's direction.

"That's right," Tom agreed, as if he were reading from a prepared script, "I've taken on an apprentice rider. Yep, I've...I've got a bug boy."

Shane's handsome face brightened. "Seems like a bit of a step-down for you, Tom. But hey, we sure could use an apprentice for our stable. Sebastian is always jammed up with horses, and it's always good to have fresh riders on hand. It's nice to get the lower weight perk, too." He turned to Dave. "We're having a bonfire at the farm tonight. Why don't you stop by and I'll introduce you to my dad and my older brother, Mike. I might be able to hook you up with some nice mounts—if you can prove you're a good rider."

Smiling, Dave extended his hand to Shane. "I appreciate that. I'll be sure to stop by."

"What did you need, Shane?" Doc asked.

"Nothing really, Dad wanted me to stop by to remind you about the bonfire. You're comin', aren't you?"

"We'll see," Doc said.

"That's exactly what I told him you'd say. Well, gotta go. Nice meeting you, Dave. See you tonight." He pointed his finger at Doc. "And you, too, Doc."

Satisfied with the old vet's unpersuasive nod, Shane left.

Dave asked, "What farm is he from?"

"Westwood," Tom said. "It belongs to Eric West and his sons. It's one of the most successful stables at the track."

"Westwood stable was not on the list of suspects in the drugging ring," David said. "Why am I trying to connect with them?"

"You weren't supposed to," Tom said, "but now that it's been offered, if you turned it down you would look suspect." His voice was filled with a chuckle. "I mean, what bug boy wouldn't want to ride for Westwood Stables?" He let out a snort. "Or have a big-time agent like me? Normally, I wouldn't waste my time with the likes of you."

"Wait a minute. West…as in Kate West? Dr. Holden Reese's girlfriend and vet assistant?"

"She hasn't got anything to do with drugging the horses, young man, that I can assure you," Doc said.

Dave studied the old horse doctor. He could see the commitment to his claim in the man's aged eyes. "I hope you're right, Doc. I hope you're right."

* * * * *

The stable area or "backside" as most horsemen called it, of Keystone Downs was quiet and all but abandoned. The Thoroughbreds were stabled in long rows known as the "shed rows.". Trainers and farms were assigned a section of the row for their horses, depending upon how many horses the farm raced and how successful the racing operation was. A paved roadway lay between the rows of stables with huge metal manure bins placed every forty feet or so. The bins were rusty and decrepit and always full. Steam rose from the fresh manure that had been dumped in the bins and the pigeons waddle around the bins picking at the oats lying about.

The morning workouts were done and most of the jockeys and exercise riders had left for the afternoon.

Shane made his way down the shed row toward the gate that led to the parking lot. It was time to head for the farm to help set up for the bonfire. Mike had sent him a text message earlier saying that he had brought in a wagonload of cord wood. Shane figured they'd be building the fire and setting up the food wagons under the very specific directions of his father's girlfriend, Jen Fleming.

As he turned the corner on the first row of stables he came upon Chip Walker and another horse trainer, Duane Bishop. Chip slipped a small package into Duane's hand which he shoved into his shirt pocket when his gaze fell upon Shane's. Quickly, the two men set off in different directions, but not before Chip tossed Shane a warning look.

What a jerk! Like that didn't look too suspicious.

After watching Chip disappear around one corner while Duane hurried around another, Shane was slipping his cell phone from his hip pocket to scroll through his text messages when he heard a ruckus behind him. He turned to see a Thoroughbred jumping and prancing in place while the rider struggled to gain control.

Snorting, the animal tossed its head from side to side while the rider spoke to the horse in Spanish. Shane glanced at the time on his phone: 11:15. All the horses should've been cooled down, groomed, and settled in their stalls by then.

Finally, the horse reared up and the rider tumbled to the pavement with a hard thud. The horse dashed down the shed row toward Shane.

Immediately, Shane spread his arms out and spoke softly to the horse, "Easy boy, easy now."

The horse stopped and snorted.

Slowly, Shane made his way toward him. The horse's eyes were as big as saucers. His nostrils were flared. His neck glistened with sweat and lather. He

27

pounded his hooves on the pavement while shaking his head.

Shane recognized the horse as Malibu Magic—a Thoroughbred who used to run under Westwood's banner. He reached for the reins, except as soon as he grabbed them the horse reared again and backed away on his hind legs.

"C'mon now, settle down, Malibu..." Shane cajoled. He could see that the animal was not in his right mind. Malibu Magic had been drugged. He was high.

Out of the blue, another pair of hands grabbed the reins from Shane's grasp. "Let the horse go!" Chip snarled.

The horse had brought his front feet back to earth, but continued to pull and fuss.

The horse not belonging to him, Shane did as Chip commanded. He let go of the reins.

The exercise rider had recovered from his fall and scurried to Chip's side.

Nervous, he told Chip in broken English, "I'm sorry, but the horse is not right. I couldn't get him back to the stable. He fought me the whole time and the pony rider...she was nowhere to be found."

"If you can't handle the job, don't come back lookin' for morning mounts at my stable!" Chip tersely told the boy. The young rider stuffed his crop into his boot and marched away.

Good call, Shane thought.

"Maybe if the horse wasn't all freaked out on drugs, the kid could do his job." Shane said.

Glaring at the youngest West, Chip shoved him. "This ain't none of your fuckin' business, West! None of it is!"

"Isn't this Malibu Magic? He didn't need drugs when he used to run for us. He was a damned good horse. Now look at him! He's nothing but a freakin' addict!" Shane bit out.

Still struggling to keep the horse in tow, Chip got in Shane's face. "Like I said, this ain't none of your concern! But just for your information, he ain't never tested positive. Now get outta my way, and if you know what's good for you'll stay outta my way!"

Chip shouldered past Shane, while fighting to keep the horse under control when he disappeared around the corner.

"I'd love to know how your horses aren't testing positive," Shane mumbled.

* * * * *

October ushered in brisk evenings accompanied by the tinge of orange and gold on the trees. Most Pennsylvanian's would readily admit that autumn is their favorite time of year. The leaves slowly drift to the ground while summer bids her rueful farewell.

Eric West leaned on the paddock fence outside the huge barn to admire the colors that surrounded Westwood Thoroughbred Farm. The golden tapestry framed her like a well fitted ball gown glittering in the rays of the setting sun. It was as if she waited to be stripped and then clad in the sparkle of white when winter came to cloak her with snow.

No matter the season, the fifty-five year old handsome patriarch of Westwood Thoroughbred farm found her to be a study in beauty and grace that embraced the long white barns with blue tin roofs, and stretches of pristine white fencing that corralled his prize Thoroughbreds. The gracious Victorian farmhouse that his family had lived in since the 1930s stood on an embankment keeping watch over the farm. The grand oaks spread their sinewy branches over the winding driveway.

She greeted the springtime with new foals, fresh sweet grasses, daffodils, and azalea's bursting with bright colors. She entertained summer with a rolling green landscape, but it was the autumn when she truly showed off her spectacular beauty.

Eric smiled at her—she was his most prized possession to be handed down to generations of Wests. She never looked as grand as she did at that moment in the dancing shadows of the bonfire surrounded by guests laughing and talking.

A pair of arms wrapped around his waist to draw him away from his thoughts and the view of the sunset. A soft feminine voice whispered, "Your party guests are over there, Mr. West."

Smiling into his chest, he said, "I was admiring the beautiful sunset. I thought women went gaga over men who enjoyed a good sunset." He turned to look into the fairy-green eyes of Jen Fleming.

The lovely brunette stretched up on her tip-toes to kiss his lips. "I am gaga over you. I just don't want your guests to think you're ignoring them."

Jen took him by the hand to lead him toward the hay wagon where several kegs of beer and a well-stocked buffet were set up. Westwood's farm manager, Punch McMinn, leaned against the wagon with his arms wrapped around his girlfriend, Zoe Miller, while having a discussion with Eric's eldest son, Mike.

The trio urged a smile from Eric. Punch was a huge black man who would intimidate anyone. The truth was that he had the heart of a teddy bear. Eric often referred to Punch as the Saint Frances of Westwood. It was the virtue that endeared the big man the most to Zoe.

Mike had grown up with Punch. They were like brothers.

Mike was almost a mirror image of his father, tall, well-built, a thick nest of dark hair, and a strong square jaw that was a West trait. Unlike his son, Eric's hair was no longer that dark—it had a spatter of gray throughout.

"I heard ol' Doug O'Conner got suspended for ninety days," Eric heard Punch say when they drew close.

"What for?" Mike turned to pour a cup of beer for his father.

"That big sorrel gelding of his that never finishes on the board won a big race the other night and then tested positive for high levels of Ketoprofen." Punch shook his head. "I don't know what the old coot was thinking."

Handing Eric the red solo cup filled with a frothy beer, Mike said, "He was thinking that he could get away with it, that's what."

Eric took a long swig of the beer. "The purses at Keystone Downs have never been so high, and the drug use has never been so prevalent."

"The money's great," Punch offered, "but it sure is bringing out the worst in everybody."

"Ha!" Mike scoffed, "I don't think that it's too hard to bring out the worst in Doug O'Conner."

Punch laughed at the thought of the crusty and cantankerous old horse trainer. Raising his cup, he said, "I'll drink to that."

As they all took a drink of their beers, Shane appeared from the shadows of the bonfire. At twenty-three, the striking sandy-haired man was the youngest of the West family. "Dad..." he called to Eric, "Did Tom Jacobs find you? He's got a bug rider with him that he wants to introduce you to."

Licking froth from his lips, Mike said, "Hmmm, we could use an apprentice rider for some of our third string horses—if he's good. Sebastian is pretty busy with the others. How much do you think he weighs?"

Shane shrugged, "He looked to go about one fifteen."

Mike exchanged questioning glances with his father.

Raising a brow, Eric said, "A fresh rider with a big time agent? This should be interesting."

Suspicion was starting to settle over the conversation when Tom Jacobs emerged from the shadows with the slightly built young man at his side.

Tom wore a greasy grin around the stubby cigar sticking out of his pudgy face. Feeling more at ease than he had that afternoon, he reached out to shake Eric's hand. The cigar moved in his lips when he spoke with his smooth southern drawl, "Eric... boys..." His eyes brightened at the sight of Jen at Eric's side. "Ms. Fleming, you're looking as beautiful as always. If you ever get tired of Eric, I'm available."

Jen rolled her eyes.

Tom's gaze moved to the dark-blonde haired woman standing next to Punch. "Who is this lovely pet?"

"Ms. Fleming isn't available at anytime, and this is Zoe Miller, Punch's girlfriend." Eric told him.

Tom removed his cigar. He took Zoe's hand to kiss it tenderly, and then he winked at her. "You like 'em big, don't cha, sweetie?"

Taken aback by Tom's offhand statement, Zoe's eyes widened. Considering the source, Punch simply shook his head.

Eric blew out an impatient breath. "What can we do for you, Tom?"

"I wanted you to meet my new man, Dave Blake. He just arrived from California, and he's looking for mounts."

Dave nodded at the West men, Punch, and the two ladies

"I told him that the Wests race only the best," Tom said. "I sure would appreciate it if you'd give Dave a shot at some of them." He flashed his smile at them, revealing a gold-capped front tooth.

Eric gauged the young man. "We always like to give the bug-boys as many opportunities as possible. Where did you ride in California?"

Looking around at the eyes that were measuring him up, Dave cleared his throat. "Santa Anita for a while. I was able to scare up a few mounts at Hollywood Park. I decided to come here for a change of scenery."

Eric flinched when Tom suddenly swatted him on the back. "C'mon, boys, you know I always take good care of the Wests. How's about it?" Tom was telling a half-truth. The Wests didn't have problems getting riders for their horses, and they mainly used Sebastian O'Terra as their lead jockey. However, Tom would waddle into the Westwood stables at Keystone Downs in the mornings to make certain that they had plenty of exercise boys to cover the morning mounts for workouts. On the rare occasions that they came up short, Tom would eagerly provide a substitute rider for the day.

Taking this into consideration, Eric said, "Come by tomorrow morning. Mike will toss you up on a few to see how you get along."

"Thank you, Mr. West," Dave said.

Tom eased past Punch and Zoe to pour himself a beer. Stuffing the cigar back into his mouth, he turned to Eric and, with a toxic grin on his lips, said, "I heard that bay gelding that you claimed from Dan Quaide won a big race last night."

Tom's comment earned him tight stares from the West men and Punch McMinn.

Dan Quaide was a burly Thoroughbred trainer with a loud mouth and an aggressive training program. He was usually on the top ten winning trainers list at Keystone Downs, yet he placed the bay gelding known as Shady Deal in a claiming race. Depending on their level, most horses are placed in claiming races that are worth anywhere from five thousand to thirty thousand dollars. Anyone can buy any horse that is entered in such races at the claiming price listed in the program.

Although Shady Deal seemed to have some minor health issues, Mike was a fan, so he went to the racing office before the race, filled out a claiming slip, and dropped it into the claiming box. After the race was over, Shady Deal was automatically the property of Westwood Stables, regardless of the outcome. Even if the horse had fallen and broken his leg during said race, Mike had made the purchase. It was a calculated risk that Eric, Mike, and Punch thought was well-worth-while.

Shady Deal did not disappoint them. He had won his first race under the Westwood Stables banner by ten lengths. Recalling the gelding's convincing victory, the right side of Eric's mouth kicked up.

Eric replied to Tom's remark, "Impressively."

Tom took the cigar from his mouth. Examining the tip between his chubby fingers, he said, "Ya know, Quaide don't like havin' his best runners claimed." He dragged his gaze toward Mike. "Even if they're claimed by his daughter's boyfriend."

It was true. Mike had been seeing Dan's daughter, Taysa.

Mike said nothing—giving Tom no satisfaction.

Lifting his chin, and folding his arms over his chest, Eric said, "Then he shouldn't run them in a claiming race."

"Maybe. Thanks for giving the kid a chance. He'll be here bright and early tomorrow morning.

I think he'll do a good job for ya." Tom winked at Jen and Zoe. "Goodnight ladies."

With that, Tom waddled toward the bonfire with Dave close behind.

Mike turned to his father. "What happened to the old, 'I'll think about it,' routine?"

Eric's eyes remained trained on Tom as he disappeared into the crowd gathered around the bonfire. "Tom Jacobs is one of the top jockey agents at Keystone. He doesn't usually mess around with bug-boys. Why is he shopping this one around at the best stables?"

Jen patted Eric's arm. "Always so suspicious. Maybe he comes recommended."

"Maybe I should make some calls to find out who he's been riding for," Eric said.

"Good idea," Mike replied. "Until things settle down a little at the track, it might be a good idea to keep a close eyes on newcomers."

"I think we should forget about this for the rest of the evening and visit with your guests," Jen said.

Eric wrapped his arm around the tiny brunette, and she placed her hand in the back pocket of his jeans to give his buttock a playful squeeze. "You're right. This whole conversation is a downer. Let's go enjoy the bonfire with our friends."

Jen smiled up him.

When they turned to go, they came face to face with Dan Quaide. The big man was not smiling.

His expression was filled with rage, and his posture was most threatening.

Jen's eyes widened. Eric stepped protectively in front of her.

Smelling of liquor, Dan swaggered from side to side. His tone was gruff and full of resentment when he said, "So, Eric, how's Shady doin'?"

"Kinda surprised to see you here tonight, Dan," Shane stepped close to his father.

"Hey, the flyer at the track said 'everyone welcome.'" Flinging his arms wide, Dan almost knocked himself to the ground. "So here I am!"

"Fair enough," Eric said. "Behave yourself and have a nice time, Dan."

Taking Jen's hand, he attempted to step past the brawny man. Dan grabbed him by the shirt. Mike and Punch rushed forward, but Eric put his hand up and pushed Jen toward the large black man, who stepped in front of her and Zoe.

Waiting for what would happen next, the tension among the small group was thick.

"I'm offerin' you fifteen thousand dollars for Shady." Dan pulled Eric closer to his face.

Disgusted by Dan's behavior and the smell of his breath, Eric pried his hands from his shirt. Dan's glance rotated toward Punch, who greeted him with a scowl.

Eric explained, "C'mon, Dan, the horse is running in thirty-thousand dollar claimers. You want me to sell him for half of that? I'll pass."

"You claimed him from me for fifteen!"

Keeping his cool demeanor, Eric locked his eyes on Dan's. "If you want him back, you can reach in and take him through the claiming box."

Dan choked out a frustrated chuckle. "You're such a bastard."

The terse conversation at the wagon had caught the attention of the crowd around the bonfire. A hush fell over the party.

"I'm a good businessman. You put him in a claiming race. I claimed him. He just won me a lot of money—after Mike and Punch spent six weeks drying him out."

Dan's face hardened. The flush began at the base of his thick neck and exploded to his cheeks. He bellowed, "Are you callin' me a cheater, West?"

"If the shoe fits—"

"I don't use nothing but herbs."

"Is that what you call them?"

Dan lunged at Eric who quickly stepped aside. The big man hit the dirt.

Gasping, Jen grabbed her forehead with both hands. Shane gathered Jen and Zoe to lead them out of harm's way behind the wagon.

Dan spit the dirt he had eaten onto the ground and then rolled over. With a crooked grin on his lips, he wiped the filth away, and pushed to his feet. Swaggering, he attempted an off-balance swing at Eric's jaw. Eric jerked sideways to avoid the punch. When he straightened, he landed a solid blow to Dan's stomach. Grunting, Dan wrapped his arms around his torso and staggered in place before falling on to his back.

Rubbing his fist, Eric walked to the keg, grabbed a red solo cup from the pile, and poured himself a fresh beer. After taking a gulp, he went back to where Dan lay in the dirt—still clutching his stomach. Standing over him, he said in a firm tone, "If you want the horse, claim him."

Punch leaned in close to Mike. He asked, "Um, how are you gonna smooth this over with Taysa?"

"I have no freaking idea."

* * * * *

The hayloft was dim. Only the few aisle lights from below that were always left on illuminated Kate's blonde hair. She sat up from the loose hay to gather her bra and her blouse that lay nearby. Holden tugged her back into his arms against his bare chest. He kissed her on the top of her head and then whispered into her ear, "You make such a sexy little cowgirl."

"I thought I was supposed to be a sassy cowgirl."

"That goes without saying. By the way, did you tell them that we're engaged?"

Kate bit her lip. "No, not yet, Holden."

"What are you waiting for? I would think that your daddy would be happy to have a veterinarian in the family."

"He will. I'm just waiting for the right time. Everyone seems so edgy with all this crap going on at the track."

Holden scrubbed his hand across his chin. "We could go to Vegas."

"I can't, Holden. Dad's going to want to walk me down the aisle. I can't take that away from him."

"Mmmm, what would Daddy do if he knew you were up here in the hayloft having sex with me?" Holden teased.

"Punch you in the nose."

"C'mon, Kate. You're twenty-six years old. You've spend the night at my apartment."

"Your point?"

Holden raised his eyebrows.

Kate giggled, "Don't worry. I'll tell them soon."

Holden snatched a piece of hay from her hair and shoved it into his mouth. He chewed on the straw while watching her cover her breasts with the bra. His cell phone vibrated in the back pocket of his jeans. Holden dug through to retrieve the phone and took note of the caller on the screen: Chip Walker.

He muttered to Kate, "Real soon, I hope."

~ TWO ~

Guido the goat scurried through the barn with a chunk of dirty straw in his teeth. Carrying his saddle down the aisle, Eric snickered at the big-bellied creature.

Guido was yet another of Punch's rescues. The goat tended to be a sore subject of conversation. Mike hated him. He was always getting into trouble and chewing things. Goats were the least of Mike's favorite animals. But Punch had drug the old Billy goat home as a stable companion for Sheldon, one of the Thoroughbreds.

The newest addition was just part and parcel to Punch's soft-hearted demeanor. The goat needed a home and their insecure Thoroughbred, Sheldon, needed a full-time stable companion. Punch decided that he'd killed two birds with one stone. Mike concluded that the goat was a pain in his ass and that Sheldon needed to "get over" his insecurity issues. Punch suggested that Mike was being too hard on Sheldon. Mike suggested that Punch take Guido to live in his apartment.

They were at an impasse.

Eric stopped by a stall where Punch was wrapping a Thoroughbred's legs. "Hey Punch, I think you should saddle up Charlatan and cover the outrider position at the other end of the track from me today. We've got that bug rider coming in, and you never know what kind of trouble that's going to cause."

"No problem," Punch said. "I sent Shane to Keystone this morning to supervise the stable chores there."

Eric glanced over his shoulder in time to see Guido spit out the slimy hunk of straw only to steal several bites of fresh green second-cut hay from another horse's stall. The horse snorted at the goat, but he simply ignored the big bay Thoroughbred and continued to enjoy the snack.

"That works." Eric opened the gate to his old Quarter Horse's stall, Ike.

It was Thursday morning. The sky was clear and the air was crisp. The Wests usually worked the Thoroughbreds at their private training track on Thursdays, Eric's favorite day of the week. He would saddle up his old buddy Ike, sit at the far end of the training track in the out-rider position, and drink coffee.

Eric was expecting some action this particular Thursday morning, because of the apprentice/bug-rider, Dave Blake. Eric and Ike's job, or Bert and Ernie as Kate often referred to them, was to wait for a horse to run away with a rider. Jumping into action, they would run the horse down, grab the reins, and bring it under control. Most Thursdays, the dynamic duo sat at the end of the track and drank coffee for two hours while the work-outs went on without a hitch. Those were the boring mornings. Ahhh, but on occasion, they would get a rowdy horse that would grab the bit and take-off out of control. Those were exciting. Even old Ike enjoyed a good chase.

"You're right on time," they heard Mike say.

Eric and Punch peered down the barn aisle to see Dave Blake standing outside of a stall. They could hear Mike's voice from inside it.

"I'm going to throw you up on Sheldon here. He's un-raced and rather green, but he's coming along very well. Let's see how the two of you get on."

"His name is Sheldon?" Dave asked as if he hadn't heard Mike correctly.

Leading the slender bay colt from the stall, Mike chuckled. "Yep, and it fits him, too. His registered name is Bazinga, but Sheldon seemed to stick."

"Okay," Dave snorted, "Sheldon it is."

Mike gave him a leg up. Leaving his feet to dangle free from the irons, he gathered his reins to tie them into a knot while Mike led him toward the barn door. Sheldon snorted at Guido as they past by. Guido let out a Baaa and then followed along behind.

"Nice goat," Dave said.

"He won't be around much longer," Mike replied loud enough for Punch to hear.

Eric turned to Punch. "We'd better get saddled up quick. It's game time."

* * * * *

The training track was fairly busy when Mike arrived with Sheldon and Dave and Guido in tow. Sheldon's ears perked, his neck arched, and he snorted at the horses galloping along the racing rail.

Dave pushed his feet into the irons while Sheldon pranced in place. "What's the plan?" he asked Mike.

"I'm only looking for a good gallop," Mike said. "He's not ready for any heat just yet. I don't want any set backs in his training like a bowed tendon."

Eric rode up to the gate on Ike with Punch at his side on Charlatan. The right side of Mike's mouth lifted at the extra reinforcements: Punch and Charlatan. He was well aware that his father had recruited Punch due to the presence of an apprentice rider on the training track.

Nodding a "good morning," they rode past in a casual manner to make it look like this was an every-day procedure.

Well played.

Once they were through the gate, Eric took a right to keep watch over the top end of the track, while Punch reined Charlatan to the left toward the lower end of the track.

The bases are covered, Mike couldn't help but think. *Game on.*

After several horses had dashed past the gate—each with a long stretch between them—and after checking that his father and Punch had taken up their positions, Mike let go of the bridle to grant Sheldon access to the track. Quickly, he grabbed Guido's collar so that he wouldn't follow. With the goat bucking and kicking, Mike drug him to a nearby tree where Punch had secured a rope so that Guido would be safely out of the way while Sheldon was galloping.

"Stupid goat," Mike muttered to himself while he attached the clip of the rope to Guido's collar.

* * * * *

Posting up and down in the tiny exercise saddle, Dave's stomach had tightened into a knot. He intended to long-trot the colt halfway up the track as a warm-up for him, and a cool-down for himself. He had spent months training for this. Yet, as the brisk breeze hit him in the face, and the horse beneath him pulled for more freedom, he felt uncertain. A lanky sorrel mare whizzed by in the passing lane. Sheldon's head jerked up. Eager to catch up, he shook it and swished his tail.

Drawing in a braced breath, Dave repeated Mike's instructions inside his head: only a good gallop. He's not ready for heat. C'mon, the directives were simple enough. He didn't have to turn in a time. He wasn't required to blow the horse out. Still, his hands were shaking. Impatience was getting the better of Sheldon. He shook his head again, and lifted his back-end in a warning buck.

Dave chuckled. "Okay, Sheldon, let's do this." He smooched to the colt, backing it up with a kick. Sheldon leapt into his gallop. The colt was smooth and happier to be moving out.

To his surprise, Dave found the exercise calming while they galloped along the rail to take in the beautiful October morning. In his peripheral vision, he saw the large black man sitting on an imposing gray Thoroughbred when he galloped past. Making the long sweeping turn to gallop down the backside of the track, he was looking at the backend of several horses many lengths ahead. Beyond the cluster of horses, he could see Eric West sitting on his Quarter Horse at the other end of the track. The Wests seemed to take safety seriously. Good idea.

Keep the horse steady and between your legs, he told himself. Many eyes were upon him, and it was important that he be accepted into the stable. Once Westwood embraced him, other trainers would come on board, and getting what he needed would become easier.

His legs were tiring by the time Sheldon approached the one-mile pole to signal the end of his gallop. Even in the brisk air, droplets of sweat trickled from under his riding helmet. It would take time to build the strength to exercise Thoroughbreds on a daily basis. He was finding out fast that this was not a job for anyone who wasn't athletic. He eased Sheldon back into a long sweeping trot to return to the gate where Mike stood watching intently.

Patting Sheldon's neck, Dave called to Mike, "He gallops effortlessly, smooth as silk."

Mike took hold of the bridle while Dave jumped down from the saddle. "You seemed to handle him okay. I'll have him at the track next week for you to work. It will be his first visit to Keystone, so you may have your hands full." He waited for Dave's response. Would he back away from the colt because he was afraid of Sheldon's inexperience? It was a telling moment.

Dave tried not to have a strong reaction to Mike's offer. "We'll be fine," he lied while patting

Sheldon's shoulder. "Won't we, buddy? Have you got anymore for me today?"

"No, not today," Mike replied. "I wanted to see how you handled Sheldon first. I may have more later. I'll call Tom if I need you."

"Good enough." Dave shook Mike's hand. "Thanks for letting me ride. I'm going to the track. Tom said he lined up a few mounts at the O'Conner stable for later this morning."

Mike raised an eyebrow. "Good luck." He handed Sheldon off to a stable hand who walked him back toward the barn to be cooled out and showered. When he turned back toward the track, Punch and Eric were riding through the gate. Both men dismounted their horses. Punch tossed a peppermint into the air. Charlatan caught it in his teeth and then hung his head low to savor the flavor. Ike's ears perked.

"You want a peppermint, Ike?" Punch pulled the candy from the pocket of his jeans and then held it out for the older Quarter Horse to take. Ike sniffed it and snorted, before deciding to give it a try. Ike's delight in the flavor urged a smile from Eric.

"Dave looked a little wobbly at times," Eric said, "but all in all he didn't do too badly with Sheldon."

Glancing over his shoulder, Mike watched Dave disappear from sight. "He's not a bad fit for Sheldon at this time." He turned to his father. "Did you make those phone calls?"

"I spoke with Bernie at Santa Anita. He's never heard of him. Same with Slick at Hollywood Park. Of course, there are a lot of bugs at those tracks. It would be easy to overlook one, I suppose."

"I'm going to keep him on Sheldon where I can keep an eye on him," Mike said.

"Dave Blake sure seems to be on your radar," Punch commented.

"Everyone's on my radar," Mike said.

Guido let out a loud "baaaa." Punch tossed him a peppermint.

* * * * *

Keystone Downs Racetrack...

Clinging to the door of the vet truck with one hand and the back of the seat with other, Kate insisted, "Slow down."

Holden drove through the parking lot toward the racetrack at a high rate of speed. The security guards waved him through.

Kate had received a call from one of the horse trainers, Duane Bishop, who said that his horse was down and unresponsive in the middle of the track. The riders had to be cleared, which held up the morning work outs and caused a major back-up in horses waiting their turn to go to the track before it was closed for race preparations.

A security guard pushed the gate open to give Holden entrance to the area. As he drove through the gate, he could see Duane and an exercise rider standing over a horse lying in the sand—dead still on the clubhouse turn.

Rolling the truck to a stop, Holden exchanged a look with Kate before they jumped from their seats. She had the vet box in hand. "What happened?" Holden asked as he approached the downed horse. "Did he fall and break his neck?"

"No, Dr. Reese," the young exercise boy said in a heavy Spanish accent, "the horse just collapsed from underneath me as we were galloping past the clubhouse."

Holden looked over his shoulder at the huge windows of the closed clubhouse, where empty tables with white linen cloths were waiting for the evening patrons. He knelt down next to the horse, but there was no cause for an exam, it was quite obvious that the gelding was dead. Holden looked up at Duane, who seemed unmoved by the incident. "Has the horse been sick, Duane?" he inquired.

Duane stuffed his hands into the pockets of his jeans. "Nope."

Taking notes, Kate raised her eyebrows.

Holden cocked his head. "No problems to speak of at all?"

Duane responded with a shake of his head, "No."

Holden probed, "He just dropped dead?"

"I figure he had a heart attack. Don't you think, Doc?" the trainer suggested in a leading manner.

Holden didn't like it. He stood. "I'm not sure, Duane. You tell me," he said, clipped.

Duane simply shrugged.

The vet continued, "There's nothing I can do for him, that's for sure. Call the wagon to pick him up. Let's go, Kate." He turned and went to the truck with Kate close behind.

As she closed the passenger's door, Kate looked across the seat. A flush had started at the base of Holden's neck and was working its way to his cheeks. His posture was stiff with stress. Her sexy, fun-loving cowboy was a tight ball of tension. "Do you think the horse had a heart attack?" she quietly asked.

Holden ran a hand through his hair. "Most likely," he said. "I'm going to drop you off at the office with this morning's slips."

"But there's really not that many—"

"Don't argue with me, Kate," he snapped. "You can do some catching up in the office. I won't be long."

Kate directed her gaze through the windshield. "Whatever. While you're out, can you stop by our stable? Shane called a little while ago. He's having a problem with a tendon on a mare. He'd like you to take a look."

Feeling badly about the sharp tone that he'd taken with her, he laid his hand on her thigh. "Will do."

* * * * *

Like a man on a mad mission, Holden marched into Chip's racing stable. "What the hell are you doing?" he demanded when he spotted Chip unsaddling a horse.

Chip handed the horse's lead to a thug-looking stable hand, who didn't like Holden's tone. He puffed out his wide chest, and shot Holden a steely look.

Chip raised his hand to calm the brute. "Easy Ramon, I've always got time for Doc Reese." A smirk spread across his handsome face.

Tossing Holden one more abrasive look, the huge man walked away with the sweaty horse.

"What's on your mind?" Chip asked the vet.

"I've got a dead horse out on the track—"

"I heard. Duane's such an asshole. Probably gave him too much. We're gonna have to cut Duane back a bit," Chip said as he carelessly hung a bridle on the tack rack.

Holden was trying to contain the anger swelling inside his chest. "What the hell happened with Doug O'Conner? I thought you said you've got all the bases covered, Chip. You take the scripts to your pal the pharmacist, he fills them, and your brother that no one knows is your brother in the test barn makes sure that none of the trainers in your program catches a positive test. Now suddenly O'Conner's on a ninety-day suspension because his horse spit a positive. What the hell gives?"

Chip laid his hand on Holden's shoulder. "You need to calm down, Doc—"

"Calm down? I want the hell out of this freakin' nightmare!" Holden batted his hand away.

"Let me explain how things work in my program: I provide a service to trainers. Their piece of shit horses win. In turn, they give me fifteen percent of the purse. But if a trainer, like Doug O'Conner, gets greedy and only donates ten percent to the cause, then bad things happen to said trainer— like a bad test result. That does two things: teaches a valuable lesson, and puts them back in place. Now, the same goes for members of my organization who decide that they no longer wish to cooperate..."

Chip's explanation was interrupted by a slice of sunshine from the barn door opening. A hulk of a man stepped inside.

"Everything okay, Parker?" Chip asked.

The man nodded before going into Chip's office.

"Who the hell is that?" Holden asked.

"That's Parker. His job is to make sure that he knows where Miss Kate West is at all times. You know, just in case your cooperation level would take a dip. I haven't been very happy with the way you've been ignoring my calls and texts."

Chip called over his shoulder, "Hey Parker, where's Miss West right now?"

From inside the office, Parker's voice boomed, "In Doc Reese's office."

Holden grabbed Chip by his shirt, slammed him against the wall, and hoisted him off his feet. He was almost nose to nose with Chip when he warned, "If you ever touch Kate, I'll kill you!"

The corner of Chip's mouth lifted. "Fall in line, Doc, and you won't ever have to worry about one blonde hair on that beautiful woman's head."

* * * * *

Chip Walker had Holden by the balls and was squeezing tight.

At this point, the young veterinarian wanted two things: Kate to marry him and to get the hell out of Dodge—not necessarily in that order. Unfortunately, the woman was so committed to her family that she refused to leave.

Holden had to bow under Chip's demands. For the moment.

Nonetheless, Holden was positive about one thing: God help Chip if any of his thugs laid one hand on his woman.

His eyes rotated to the clock on the dashboard: 10:30. The morning was getting old and he still had some rounds to do. Kate had asked him to stop by Westwood Stables to check on a mare with a pulled tendon.

Holden started the truck and let it slowly roll along the shed rows. Trying to calm down, he nodded at several exercise girls strolling along with coffee cups in hand. They were twirling their crops through their fingers. Further along, he waved at Dan Quaide while the trainer steadied a horse for a jockey who was jumping off.

Chip had never informed him of which trainers participated in his "program," and he wasn't sure that he wanted to know. Nevertheless, he found himself looking at each and every one with feelings of distrust, suspicion, and disdain. Everyone was suspect.

Moreover, everyone was guilty—Duane Bishop was a definite.

Finally, weaving in and out of the shed rows, he rolled the truck to a stop in front of Westwood Stables.

Grabbing his vet box, he slid from the driver's seat and made his way to the stable door just as Tom Jacobs was stepping out. Tom's stubby cigar was perched at the corner of his lip. It glowed like a third eye bulging out of his chubby face. Tom eyed the young vet. Without saying a word, he tugged the cigar from his mouth, pitched it at Holden's feet, stomped it out hard, and then shouldered past him.

Through his sunglasses, Holden watched Tom walk down the shed row until he turned the corner. Pushing the glasses onto his head, he pressed through the barn door to make his way down the aisle.

The horses peeked at him from their stalls as he past. A few laid their ears against their heads and nipped at him, while others ducked into their stalls. They were well aware that he was the vet.

Holden found Shane in a stall toward the end of the aisle rubbing down a mare's leg. He rapped on the stall wall. "Hey, Shane, how's tricks?"

Shane glanced over his shoulder. "Not too bad. How about you?"

"Don't you think you ought to leave the vet work up to the vet?"

Shane snorted. "What vet?"

"Ba-ha-ha, you're so damned funny."

Grabbing the rag hanging from his hip pocket, Shane stood up and wiped his hands. "I heard that one of Duane Bishop's horses dropped dead on the track this morning. One too many cocktails?"

"News travels fast."

"Very fast," Shane agreed. "Are you going to do an autopsy?"

"What? Hell no. What for?"

Tossing the rag onto a bale of straw, Shane stepped from the stall. "Oh, I dunno, maybe to find out what Bishop's using," he bit out.

At the far end of the barn, Chip stepped through the door—unnoticed. He quietly leaned against the wall, out of the way, but well within a comfortable hearing distance.

"I don't think that an autopsy is called for. The horse probably had a heart attack," Holden said.

"Let me get this straight. As a track vet, you think it's just best to look the other way? I'll bet Doc Spears won't feel that way."

"Don't you think I've got enough to do around here? Will the stewards be informed? You bet! But am I going to go out of my way to bust someone for a bad morning? No freakin' way! Spears can do whatever the hell his wants!"

"What's the matter, Holden? Are you afraid to blow the whistle on these guys? You seem to be cozy with Chip Walker. Oh yeah, there's a real upstanding horseman. I wouldn't be surprised if he was at the top of the drug lord totem pole," Shane said with a growl.

Dropping his chin to his chest, Holden drew in a deep breath. This was Kate's brother. He needed to tread carefully.

A voice from the end of the barn called out, "Hey, Shane..."

They turned to find Chip approaching them. A wide grin crossed his face.

What the hell is he doing here? Shane thought.

Holden's shoulders tightened.

Chip nodded at him. "Doc Reese..."

Put-off by the visitor, Shane dropped the terse conversation. "What's up, Chip?"

"I saw the Doc's truck outside. I could use some DMSO," Chip turned to Holden. "You got any?"

Holden's jaw was so tight that the skin rippled over the bone. "Yeah, I've got some in the truck," he said before asking Shane, "Do you need me to look at that mare?"

"I got it covered," Shane said, clipped.

Holden held eye contact with the youngest West for a moment. He didn't miss the reprimand and the disapproval in his expression. He turned and marched toward the door, which he slammed as he exited.

Tossing Shane a quick nod, Chip hurried through the barn to catch up. When he stepped through the barn door, he bumped into a young rider that he'd never seen before. The young man grabbed his arm to steady him.

"Sorry," Dave Blake said.

"No problem," Chip muttered while giving the rider a quick once-over. Dismissing him as inconsequential, Chip proceeded toward Holden's truck.

Twirling his crop through his fingers, Dave strolled down the shed row a short distance until he found a post to lean against to watch Chip Walker and Dr. Holden Reese.

When Chip reached the vet truck, Holden spun to face him. Flushed with irritation, his voice was low and threatening. "Don't follow me to the West's stable. I don't want them drawing any parallels between you and me. They're getting more suspicious every day. You heard Shane."

Chip's lips lifted into a poisonous smile. "Don't worry. The West's will back off. You'll see."

Holden grabbed Chip by the T-shirt. "What the hell is that supposed to mean?"

Brushing Holden's hand away, Chip said, "Don't worry they'll get the message loud and clear and the Brady Bunch will still be intact. Do what you're told, Doc. I'll take care of the rest."

Wiping his mouth with the back of his hand, Holden looked up to find Doc Spears sitting in his vet truck across the shed row. The old vet was watching them. Holden bit down on his lip as he yanked the truck door open, hopped inside, and drove slowly down the shed row past Dave Blake, who nodded at him.

* * * * *

A half-hour later, Dave was relieved to be pressing through the door of a dinky apartment in the low-rent section of Rosemount. He pinched back the moth-bitten drapes on the window to check the street below. Two rough-looking characters were exchanging money on the street corner. A woman carrying a bag of groceries in one arm and a baby in the other circled wide to avoid them on her way to the apartment building. Too exhausted to care, he let the drape fall back into place. Rubbing his lower back, he shuffled to the threadbare couch along the wall across from an ancient analog TV.

As he dropped onto the couch, his cell phone rang. He pulled the cell from his pocket, "Dave Blake..."

"Mike West called. He's gonna keep you on their bay colt, Bazinga. He wants you back at the farm in the morning to ride him one more time before he goes to the track," Tom Jacobs told him. "Like I said, riding for Westwood is gonna open doors to other stables that would normally slam it shut on a newbie's face. Ridin' for the Wests will give you credibility real quick. Don't make me regret it, okay?" And with that, Tom abruptly hung up.

Tossing the cell aside, Dave pulled his dusty T-shirt over his head and pitched it to the floor. Grunting, he yanked his riding boots from his feet and flung them across the room. Dust fell from the boots when they hit the wall and bounced to the carpet. Lying back against the couch, he stared up at the yellow stains that ran along the cracks of the ceiling. The ceiling fan whirled the stale air around the room. He pressed his eyes closed while running his fingers through his hair and over the back of his stiff neck.

Letting out a ragged breath, he picked up the cell and thumbed the numbers on the pad. He listened to it ring on the other end. Finally, someone answered, "How'd it go?"

"I'm in," Dave said.

"Any problems?"

"No problems. Jacobs sent me to Westwood stable. He said that it should open a lot of doors. I'll call you at the end of the week."

"Good. Kate West works for Dr. Reese. Keep me in the loop."

The line went dead.

Dave thumbed the END button.

Thoughtfully, he eyed the weight bench sitting across the room. He needed to pick up his weight training to build more stamina. Instead, he picked up the remote for the TV. He was thinking that Shane West would be a good ally to have.

~ THREE ~

Dave parked an aged Grand Am in front of the barn at Westwood Thoroughbred Farm. The car's door moaned and groaned and felt as if it would fall from its hinges when he shouldered it open. A real piece of crap, it was only temporary.

He took in the vast farm. He would have looked around when he rode Sheldon the other day, but his nerves had gotten the best of him. Now he could appreciate how beautiful the Thoroughbred farm was. Feeling good in the fresh autumn air, young Thoroughbreds kicked, bucked, and galloped through a nearby paddock. The leaves on the trees were starting to turn subtle shades of yellow and orange. A Victorian farmhouse stood proudly on a hillside overlooking the barns and paddocks. A stone bungalow rested on the other side of the farmhouse. The cottage had curtains and hanging baskets on the porch.

Dave took note of the buildings and the layout before he made his way into the barn.

When he stepped through the barn door, he found a stable hand lugging two buckets down the aisle while another was gathering a wheelbarrow and a pitchfork. Bales of hay were neatly stacked along the wall of the aisle. The smell of freshly broken bales filled his nostrils. Almost in harmony to the horses bumping around feed buckets from inside their stalls, Reba McEntire's voice wafted throughout the barn.

When the stable hand with the buckets drew closer, Dave asked, "Any of the Wests around?"

"I saw Shane a little bit ago. He was going into stall number fourteen," he replied in a heavy Spanish accent.

"Thanks." Dave strolled down the aisle, patting horses along the way, until he came to stall fourteen.

Shane was humming along with the Reba while cleaning Sheldon's hoof with a pick.

"Hey Shane," Dave called to him.

Surprised by his presence, Shane straightened.

"I know I'm really early, but I'm here to ride Sheldon."

"Oh, no one told me," Shane said. "No problem, I can saddle him right up for you." He gathered a saddle and bridle, and prepped Sheldon for a morning gallop.

While Dave tied the reins in a knot up in the saddle, Shane led Sheldon down the path to the training track. "Where do you go around here for a cold beer and some fun?" he asked in a casual tone.

"Depends on what kind of fun you're looking for," Shane replied. "The beer is always cold at Barney's Bar and Grill. My buddies and I like to play pool, plus a lot of pretty girls hang out there, too."

"Sounds good. What about the Post Time Bar at the track?"

"I go there sometimes, usually after the races. It's a dive, but the beer's always cold."

"You're not mentioning the girls," Dave pointed out.

"Eh, it's mostly old jockeys and even older patrons," Shane explained.

Dave laughed.

"I've only got one mount tonight, in the fifth race," Dave said. "I saw on the board that you've got one in the second. How about we meet up at your stable after the fifth and we'll drive over to Barney's?"

"You play pool?"

"I like pretty girls."

"You're on," Shane said.

They had arrived at the gate to the training track. Sheldon's ears perked and his neck arched.

"Okay Sheldon," Dave said. "I won't keep you waiting today. Let's go." He urged the colt forward.

* * * * *

After Sheldon was returned to his stall, Dave firmed-up his evening plans with Shane and then made his way to the barn door. He noticed Mike sitting in the office with his legs propped up on the desk. He held a small bottle in one hand while reading a sheet of paper in the other. Dave had managed to make friends with the youngest West. This could be a prime opportunity to make nice with his older brother.

Stepping through the door, Dave said, "Hey, Mike."

Mike glanced up from the paper. "Hey, how'd it go?"

"He's doing really well. I like him a lot."

"Good to hear." Mike glanced at the clock on the wall. "You sure did get in early this morning."

"Yeah, I've got horses waiting for me at the track," Dave explained. "So I figured I'd stop here as early as possible. I've picked up some mounts for Dan Quaide and Duane Bishop."

Mike cocked his head to one side, his eyes narrowed.

Dave asked, "What's wrong?"

"I'm just surprised at the stables that you've picked up: O'Conner and Bishop."

"I gotta get mounts where I can," Dave said. "I need the experience if I ever want to be a professional jockey, right?"

"I suppose."

Mike's stare seemed to be probing.

Dave changed the subject. "What are you reading?"

Mike tossed the bottle into his hands. "It's a new bottle of herbs that I need to clear through the vet before I use them. Unfortunately, I don't have time to check on this one before tonight's race."

Studying the label on the bottle, Dave lifted a shoulder. "I wouldn't worry too much about it. They only test for Phenylbutazone and Clenbuterol on Fridays. So if you win, they won't even be looking for this stuff." He pitched the bottle back to Mike. "Don't you have one in on Saturday, too?"

"Yeah..."

"I'd say you're good to go." Dave tossed Mike a wink as he stepped away from the office to stroll toward the barn door. He patted horses as he past. Punch was coming into the barn as Dave was going out. "Mornin', Punch."

"Morning." Punch checked his watch. He found Mike leaning against the door jamb of his office. "He sure does get things done early."

"He gets things done all right," Mike said. "O'Conner and Bishop. What do these three trainers have in common?"

"Better racing through chemistry. What's up?"

"I'm not sure, but I've got a few questions about our new bug boy," Mike said.

* * * * *

Keystone Downs Racetrack...

Dr. Ben Spears sat in his vet truck at the end of the shed row on the backside of Keystone Downs. He had spent the last thirty years making morning rounds at the track ever since his early years as a vet. Now, his hair was white, he walked with a stiff limp, and he possessed a crotchety demeanor.

Nevertheless, the people of Keystone were his family, and he kept a close eye on the goings-on. Not too much slipped past the old horse doctor. Even though he was busy filling out a form, he had an eagle eye on Chip Walker's stable.

Ava West, Doc Spears' vet assistant, jumped into the truck and tossed her auburn hair over her shoulder. "Okay, I put the blood samples in the back, and Vince finally paid his bill." She placed the check in the money box on the seat.

Holden Reese's vet truck grabbed Ava and Doc's attention when it pulled up to Chip's stable. Kate was not in the passenger's seat.

A moment later, Chip strutted from the barn to the truck with two huge goons at his heels.

Ava shot a glance at Doc. He let out a low grouse.

Holden let down his window, and the two men appeared to have a fiery exchange. Chip's hands waved about as if he was trying to get some point across to the young vet, but Holden didn't seem to see things his way.

Chip's temper blew. He punched the door of the vet truck.

Ava flinched at the sight.

Doc let out a breath.

The two big thugs drew closer to the truck.

Ava drew her hand to her lips.

They watched intently.

Holden appeared to be writing something. He tossed a slip out the window at Chip and then drove off.

Chip flipped a rude gesture in the direction of the truck, and yet he seemed satisfied with what Holden had given him. He and the thugs went back into the stable.

Ava turned to Doc. "What was that all about?"

"Nothing good."

"I wonder where Kate is."

"Let's find out." The old vet shoved the truck into gear to roll through the shed rows until he turned the corner of row B, where Dr. Reese's office was located.

The veterinarian offices were tucked between stables along the shed rows and built of the same cement blocks. The interior walls had been painted a dull white, and the floors were cement. There were no windows, and the solid door was heavily secured with a good quality dead bolt. The vets usually kept shelving units along one wall to hold an inventory of medical supplies and a small table with a coffee maker. A simple metal desk in the middle of the room, were the only items that filled the dank office space. The real perk was that the vets had a private bathroom.

Shoving the gear shift into PARK, Doc looked across the seat at Ava. "Are you comin'?"

Rolling her eyes, Ava snorted. "Yeah...right."

Chuckling, Doc Spears slid from the seat. There was no way Ava West was going to visit with Kate West. Ava was Mike's ex-wife. She was a beautiful woman with long sexy legs and green bedroom eyes that had made an appearance in many men's bedrooms—including Dr. Holden Reese.

Nowadays, Ava had taken up with Lieutenant Carl Lugowski of the Rosemount Police Department. That didn't mean she had become Miss Fidelity. Ava was a manipulator first and foremost. A devoted girlfriend, wife, or lover was not part of Ava's repertoire.

Doc hobbled to the door of Holden's office. After giving it a good solid rap, he pressed through to find

Kate leaning on an elbow with her hand holding up her cheek behind her desk.

When she saw the old doctor, she sat up. "Good morning, Ben. What brings you by?"

"I'm surprised to find you in the office, Kate. I thought you'd be out on rounds with Dr. Reese."

"Holden had some errands to run," she said. "He left me here to catch up on paperwork, only I've been completely caught up for days. I would've gotten more done if I'd just worked at the farm today."

Doc noted a trace of complaint in her voice. "I just saw him at Walker's stable. I notice he spends a lot of time there."

Kate hesitated. Her eyes narrowed, yet she rationalized, "Well, Chip's got a lot of horses."

"If you have questions about my rounds, Dr. Spears," Holden said from the doorway, "you should ask me, not my assistant."

Unruffled by Holden's sudden appearance, Doc turned toward the door. "Should I be questioning your client list, Dr. Reese?"

"My client list is none of you business, and I don't want you stopping by my office in my absence," Holden said. His tone was terse, and his eyes were seething.

Standing, Kate scolded, "Holden..."

"It's okay, Kate," Doc said. "I've got rounds to do. Take care." He made his way to the door.

Holden stepped aside to allow for his exit. When Doc was beyond the door, Holden closed it and turned to Kate, who was looking at him like he'd just kicked a puppy.

Holden took a calming breath before he spoke. "It's a little upsetting how everyone loves to get up into our business, Kate."

"He's been a friend of the family forever—"

"Everyone seems to be a friend of your family," Holden said with a growl. "Everyone seems to want to know what we're doing every minute."

"That's not true."

Holden raced around the desk, grabbed her by the shoulders, and pressed her against the wall. He covered her lips with his—hard. When he drew away from the kiss, he looked into her questioning eyes. "Let's go somewhere where no one knows us. I've got a nice bundle of cash set aside. We can open a veterinary clinic in a new place. Make new friends who don't know your dress size or my shoe size. C'mon, Kate, what do you say?"

She searched his face. She loved his brown eyes, yet there seemed to be a hint of desperation lurking in them. "Holden...if you don't want to work at the track that's fine, but we don't have to go far away to open a clinic, we can open one in Rosemount."

"Have you told your family that we want to get married?"

Kate's mouth dangled open. She searched for the right words, but none seemed to surface. "Um, well..."

"You haven't."

"Not yet—"

"That's it! I'm coming over later to have a talk with your father, and then we're setting a date. You've got the rest of the day off."

Kate tried to speak, but his lips came crashing over hers. Probing, his tongue pressed inside. His hands found their way under her shirt, up her tummy, and over her ribs to caress her breasts over the smooth satin bra.

"Don't argue with me, Miss West. I'm giving you the afternoon off, now go home." He pulled her into his embrace, pressing his lips to hers, and then he laid her across the desk. "Mmmm, and yet I'm not ready to let you go, just yet."

* * * * *

Holden's spontaneous love-making always left Kate feeling sensual, fulfilled, and replete. He satisfied every cell in her body.

Yet, even after the hot sex they had shared on the desk a short while ago, she found herself feeling more unsettled than anything else. Instead of driving straight home, Kate went to the mall to do some window shopping and even stopped by Monique's Wedding Designs in downtown

Rosemount to make an appointment to try on gowns.

She couldn't shake the uneasy feeling that Doc's visit that morning in Holden's office had caused. His words wouldn't leave her mind. *"I saw him at Walker's stable. I notice he spends a lot of time there."*

Kate didn't understand. When she and Holden drove throughout the backside of the track on rounds, they never stopped at Walker Stables. Chip Walker was never listed on her morning roster. When was Holden spending time at his stables? Furthermore, she never cashed or registered a check or payment from Chip's stable into Holden's spreadsheets.

What the hell?

It was late afternoon by the time Kate drove her red Mustang convertible through the stone entrance of Westwood. It wouldn't be long until she would have to put the roof up on the car for the winter months. The grand oaks provided a canopy of shade while she rolled along the winding drive-way to stop at the main door of the barn.

Closing her eyes, she leaned her head against the headrest. She was more than an hour late for her afternoon check of the horses at Westwood, but damn, she needed a quiet moment to think...

Six months ago Kate worried that Holden's mood swings had to do with her ex-sister-in-law, Ava. In fact, she was right. They had an affair.

Kate was crushed, but Holden was committed to making their relationship whole again.

She was so happy when he had proposed three weeks ago, yet Holden's mood swings had taken an ugly return.

It had nothing to do with Ava. Was something going on with Chip Walker? What was Holden keeping from her?

Oh, yes, Kate had heard the whispers throughout the track, and even at her own dinner table, that Chip was a cheater. Perhaps Holden knew that she didn't like him. Maybe that's why Holden didn't talk about his friendship with Chip and treated his horses while she was in the office doing paperwork.

Seriously? It was like he was a little boy hiding his friendship with the local bad boy from his mommy.

She let out a long breath.

Kate didn't like that scenario at all. She needed to have a talk with her sexy cowboy.

Secrets were not acceptable in their relationship.

She opened her eyes.

Why was she suspecting her fiancé? Perhaps he has stopped to talk to Chip several times, and Doc saw him. Now the seed of distrust was planted in her head. That's not a good thing. Doubt was another thing that is not acceptable in their relationship.

Maybe Holden was right. There were too many people up in their business.

Her thoughts were shattered by a tap on her windshield. Flinching, she looked up to find Punch, flaunting a silly toothy grin, pressed against the glass. She giggled at his antics.

"What's goin' on, girl?" the huge black man asked.

"Nothing. Sorry I'm late."

"No worries. I put a poultice on Shady Deal's left front leg."

"Is he hurting?"

"Just some damage control." He could see that something had Kate in a tangle. He asked, "Are you hurting?"

Kate smiled at her insightful friend. He always knew. Dragging the band that held her ponytail in place from her hair, she uttered a deep sigh. "I've got a lot on my mind. I need some time to sort things out a bit."

Punch grabbed the latch on her door and pulled it open. "I've got just the thing you need. C'mon."

Kate cocked her head at him.

He hitched his chin toward the barn. Smiling, she slipped from her car and followed him into the barn. He disappeared into the tack room and then emerged with a saddle over his shoulder, a saddle pad in his hand, and bridle draped over his arm.

"I was just about to take Charlie for a ride. I'll saddle up Ike, and you can come along. A nice long trail ride always clears my head, and I'll bet you'll see things a whole lot clearer after you've been on the back of a horse." He opened the gate to Ike's stall.

"Sounds like a good idea," Kate said.

A few minutes later, Punch and Kate were leading the two geldings down the barn aisle and out the door. They mounted the horses and with Punch and Charlatan in the lead, they moseyed down the path toward the training track.

The rich colors of fall and the soft breeze dancing through her hair already had Kate feeling at ease.

Maybe she'd been making too much of Doc's comments. Maybe she'd been over-analyzing it. Deciding to sit back and enjoy the ride, she reached down and patted Ike's neck. He was a good ole boy, and there was no question why her father enjoyed every moment that he spent on the old horse's back. She certainly enjoyed her old Quarter Horse mare, Millie. Like Ike, she was a good horse, a good friend, but Kate simply didn't have the time to devote to the horse, so she sold her to a little girl several years ago. It was best, and every year the little girl sent her a Christmas card with a picture of Millie at a horse show. The horse was being used, and that was a good thing.

Kate was surprised that her father hadn't been able to convince Jen to go riding. She had a feeling that it would happen sooner or later. Breathing in the autumn afternoon, she thought, *Jen doesn't know what she's missing.*

The tall grasses raked along the bottom of their stirrups as they rode through the field beyond the training track toward the wooded area of the farm.

Punch pointed to his far right at a group of doe staring at them with their tails in the air and their ears perked. Ignoring the deer, Charlatan and Ike plodded along. Their presence was no surprise to the horses. The deer went back to munching the grass when they realized that the horses and their riders were of no threat.

Out of the blue, they heard a *"baaaa"* rising up from the tall weeds behind them. Kate looked over her shoulder to see Guido following along. He was chewing on the bristly ends of the weeds as he traveled.

"Guido's following us," she called to Punch.

"He usually does."

"But I thought he stayed with Sheldon in the stall."

"Not always."

Kate's eyes narrowed. "But I thought poor insecure Sheldon needed Guido as a constant companion."

"Not really," Punch replied. "He's mainly here until I can find a good home for him and to annoy the shit out of Mike. It does my heart good to watch him drag Guido to and from the training track when Sheldon could give a care less if the goat is there or not."

"You should be ashamed, Mr. McMinn!" Kate said as if she were truly affronted.

"Ahhh, Mike could use a little shaking up... it builds character," Punch said with a laugh in his voice.

"Mike could use a good woman in his life," Kate noted.

"I think Zoe is working on that."

"Mmm, after the fight at the bonfire the other night, I'd be surprised if Taysa wants anything to do with Mike or our family."

"It was a setback no doubt. But I've got my money down on Zoe."

As they rode along, Kate noticed the complete look of contentment on her good friend's face. Punch looked happy, and she didn't have to think terribly hard to understand why. She urged Ike to catch up with Charlatan until they were side by side. "How are things with Zoe?"

The corners of Punch's mouth kicked up. "You're just pleased as punch with yourself, aren't you?"

Kate laughed. "I told you that Zoe Miller was perfect for you, but you wouldn't listen. I thought

someone was gonna have to hit you over the head...
Oh that's right! Someone did have to hit you over
the head."

Punch tossed her a knowing look as he scrubbed
his fingers over the back of his head where he'd been

pistol whipped a few months before. "Hey, I never
said I wasn't hardheaded."

"No, you didn't, and it's a good thing that you
are, too. Soooo, things are working out then?"

He smiled at the blonde match-maker wearing
a salacious curl on her lips. "Yep," he said. "How
about you? Does this 'sorting out' that you need to
do involve Holden?"

Kate dropped her gaze to the saddle horn. Her
lips no longer curled and the salacious playful
expression she wore but a moment ago had dissi-
pated. All of her doubts and questions came flood-
ing back. Quietly, she asked, "Have you ever seen
Holden at Chip Walker's stable?"

"I have."

She lifted her face to look him in the eye. "Often?"

"Often enough."

"Do you believe what everyone says about Chip?
That he's a cheater?"

Punch was silent. He was weighing his answer.
Finally, he replied, "I think it is a strong possibility,
yes."

"Do you think that's why Holden hides the fact that he's friends with or that he vets Chip's horses from me?"

"That's a question you'll have to ask Holden."

"It certainly is."

* * * * *

Eric pushed the empty plate that had held his sandwich across the breakfast bar, picked up his coffee cup, and opened the newspaper to an article about a young woman who had been kidnapped by her estranged lover. The police had to kill him in order to rescue her. His cell phone rang. Tossing the newspaper to the counter, he scrubbed his fingers over his chin while digging for the cell in his pocket. Finally, he lifted it to his face. "Hello..."

"Eric...it's Ben," Doc Spears said, "I gotta talk to you about Kate."

"She's okay, isn't she? Nothings happened down at the track?"

"No, she fine." Doc took in a hesitant breath. "I just think you outta keep an eye on her and that Reese boy. I'm thinking he's a dirty vet. I wouldn't want to see her get into any trouble."

Eric's eyes narrowed. His jaw tightened. "What makes you say this, Ben?"

"I wish I could, but I can't say anymore."

"What's going on?"

"Just trust me on this," Doc said. The line went dead.

A dark feeling scraped through Eric. Wondering what his old friend was talking about, he set the phone on the counter.

The worry for his daughter began.

"Who was that?" Kate asked from the dining room.

Surprised, he looked up as Kate walked across the kitchen to the fridge to pull out a bottle of water. With a shrug, he said, "Telemarketer. What's going on in Kate's world?"

She slid onto a stool next to him. "I wanted to talk to you." She drew in a deep breath, and then with a shy smile. "Holden and I are getting married."

Saying nothing, Eric dropped his gaze to the newspaper on the counter that displayed the picture of the young woman and her now deceased boy-friend. His conversation with Doc Spears replayed in his head.

His thoughts were diminished by Kate's question. "Aren't you happy for us?"

Eric shook off his apprehension. He didn't want to ruin this moment for his daughter. He managed a smile. "Of course, I'm just a little tired."

"You're all right? This couldn't have been a surprise."

"Not at all, I'm happy for you. How about a hug?"

Kate lunged into her father's arms and squeezed him with all her might. "I've already made an appointment to look at wedding dresses." She kissed him on the cheek. "Well, I'd better get cleaned up, it's almost time for lassix rounds at the track, and Holden will be waiting for me." She kissed him again and then hurried from the room.

Eric ran a hand through his hair.

In general, he liked Holden Reese. He seemed good for Kate, and whatever problems they were having several months ago seemed to have been worked out or smoothed over. His daughter appeared to be genuinely happy and in love with the man. So, he was comfortable with the relationship, except Doc's recent declaration that Holden could be a dirty vet made his insides twist.

He heard the water crashing against the shower walls above his head. He was pouring another cup of coffee when there was a knock at the front door. With coffee in hand, Eric made his way to the door to find the subject of his thoughts standing on the other side: Holden Reese.

"Hey Eric, I was hoping to catch you at home. I'd like to talk with you if I could," Holden said.

Eric managed a svelte smile. "Sure, come in."

They made their way into the study.

Holden asked. "I saw Kate's car in the drive, is she upstairs?"

"She's showering." Eric gestured for Holden to have a seat on the sofa. Only Eric did not sit next to him, nor did he take a welcoming position in one of the wing-backed chairs. Instead, he sat behind his large cherry desk, set his coffee aside, and folded his hands on the desk in an all business-like posture.

Holden fidgeted. This wasn't going to be as easy as he had expected. The look on Eric's face was stiff—almost menacing.

Then, he heard something that he'd only been warned about: the Eric West "tone," when he said, "What's on your mind, Dr. Reese?"

Oh yeah, that had to be it—it wasn't quite a bellow, and it wasn't exactly terse or even clipped. It had a sound all its own. The message was perfectly clear: Don't screw with me. The man backed up his tone with an expression that was...impressively intimidating.

Holden was suddenly feeling like he was visiting with a parole officer rather than his future father-in-law. His throat was dry. He could feel beads of sweat forming on the back of his neck.

Meanwhile, Eric and his impressively intimidating expression were waiting for his response.

"Well..." he began, uncertain of the words that he had planned to say. "As you know...I've been seeing your daughter for quite some time..."

Still Eric gauged him with that look. He hadn't let down his guard one little bit. He hadn't moved.

He hadn't blinked. It was almost as if the man wasn't even breathing.

Holden felt pressured to do better. "I would like to ask you for your blessing to marry her...sir."

Eric said nothing. He reached down and opened a desk drawer. He placed a small box on the desk and then a Glock 19. He opened the box and took out a small rag and a bottle of cleaning solvent. As if he were completely alone in the room, he squirted a miniscule amount of solvent on the rag and began wiping down the gun.

"If you want a good wife, marry one that has been a good daughter," Eric said. He did not look up from his task. "I think that's how the saying goes— although I'm not sure who said it. I can tell you that Kate is not only a good daughter, she is the best I could have ever been blessed with."

He began to clean the empty chamber of the Glock, while continuing. "She deserves only the best: a good man, a strong man, and, of course, a man of integrity."

Pausing, he looked Holden square in the eye. "Are you a man of integrity, Dr. Reese?"

Holden was taken aback. Not only was the infamous tone flowing from the man's mouth, it was almost as if Eric's eyes were lasers searing into his soul, and it was making him itch from within. He was talking about Chip Walker. That's what this was about, Chip Walker. Okay, he got the message loud and clear: if you want my blessing, hell if you want my daughter, break your ties with that sleaze-ball, Chip Walker. Easier said than done.

"Dr. Reese..."

Realizing that Eric had been waiting for his response for quite some time, Holden looked up. He probably expected an affirmative answer to the integrity question immediately, and now that Holden had zoned out on him, a solid *yes I'm a man of integrity* wouldn't come off as credible. On the other hand, what was he supposed to say? *No, Mr. West I am not a man of integrity, rather I'm a slime-wad that's been up to no good, and oh, by the way I've been sleeping with your daughter, too.*

Holden cleared his throat. "I think I am a man of integrity, Mr. West. But more importantly, I love Kate, and I will take very good care of her."

"You had better, Dr. Reese. You had better."

~ FOUR ~

The pony led Dave and his mount toward the gate. His was the fourth horse to be loaded. That meant Dave's horse had to patiently wait for six more to enter their post positions while standing in that cage. Tight quarters. Claustrophobic. The pony-girl handed the reins off to a member of the gate crew, and with unerring haste he guided Dave's mount into his post and then closed the stall gate behind him.

This was it.

Dropping his goggles into place, Dave tried to calm the hornet's nest that was rumbling through his gut. He pressed his feet into the irons and took hold of the reins.

The caging all around him clanged as the gates of the other posts where slammed closed and the horses, including his own mount, fussed. The

Thoroughbred beneath him didn't seem like he wanted to wait for the gate to open or the bells to ring. He wanted to burst forward. He danced in place, snorted, and shook his head.

Dave patted his mount's neck. "Easy now," he muttered while stealing a peek at the jockey in the next post position.

He pitched Dave a confident grin before parking his goggles onto his nose.

Glancing down through the caging, the other jockeys seemed at ease in the gate. They checked their equipment and chatted back and forth in Spanish. Sure, they'd done this a million times over.

For Dave, this was his first actual horse race. Shit, the horse knew more than he did. He'd been in test races at the training tracks where they prepped him for several months, but this wasn't a test. This was the real McCoy, and he was scared out of his mind.

Hey, it wasn't easy being a professional liar.

He'd spent his youth rounding up cows on the back of a horse. He knew how to ride, but this was a whole other animal. Was he up to the task? He was about to find out.

The last horse was pushed into his post and secured. The bells rang. The gates burst open like an explosion in front of him, and his mount surged forward. The sound of galloping hooves pounding into the sand and pitching it into the air to smack his goggles surrounded him. The horses barreled forward ahead of him as they approached the turn. Dave's mount was breathing hard. The gelding lugged to the outside and bumped the number five horse. The jockey shouted something in Spanish at him when the number five horse stumbled but managed to regain his footing. Dave didn't understand what the jockey said in what seemed to be mayhem of horses, hooves, flying sand, and pounding speed.

It didn't matter.

They were approaching the top of the stretch, and much to Dave's surprise he was riding in the middle of the pack. It was not of his doing, but rather of his mount. At the top of the stretch, the sound of the crowd became louder and louder with each hammering stride.

The front runners pulled farther away. The pack spread out like balls on a pool table. Dave was managing to hold on to fifth place, but he pulled the crop from his boot to ensure his position. Hands shaking, he cracked the crop across the horse's rump. The horse reacted by taking his stride to a higher gear.

Through the grit that had collected on his goggles, he could barely make out the finish line.

Dang, he was going to make it! Moreover he was going to hit the board—taking a forth place!

To the boisterous cheers from the crowd, the horses thundered across the finish line. The flash of the photographer's camera burst when the first horse arrived. Dave let out the breath he'd been holding throughout the race, or had he been holding his breath since the post parade? He wasn't sure, he was just happy that he made it through in one piece.

His mount slowed to an easy gallop. The horse was well aware that the race was over.

Dave stood in the stirrups to ride it out while still catching his breath when the number five horse galloped past. The jockey was pointing his crop at him while cursing in Spanish, most likely yelling something like: "Learn how to ride, asshole!"

He couldn't blame him.

* * * * *

After a long hot shower to steady his nerves, Dave shrugged into a clean V-neck T-shirt and a pair of faded ripped jeans. Gathering up his duffle bag, he left the jockey's locker room to make his way to Westwood stables on the backside of Keystone Downs where he found Shane waiting for him sitting on a bale of hay.

"About time you showed up." Standing, he made a show of taking a big whiff of Dave. "Don't you smell pretty?"

"You said there'd be girls."

"I did, didn't I?" Shane remarked as they turned off the stable lights to step out into the shed rows.

In the distance, they could hear the call for the race that was taking place on the track. The barn cats, who sunned themselves during the day, were now darting in and out of the shadows on the hunt for rats.

"Have you bumped into Ginger LaFond yet?" Shane asked as they strolled past the manure bins and darkened stables.

"I've heard her name around the track, but I haven't met her yet," Dave said.

"She's a jock. She comes into Barney's every once in a while. She's a mean little thing." Shane raised his brows with a snarky smile on his lips. "She likes handcuffs."

They pushed through the gate to approach his Jeep in the parking lot.

Dave grew a spicy grin. "You mean she likes to be cuffed to the bed?"

Shane snorted. "Other way around, dude."

Dave came to a dead stop. With a chuckle in his voice, he declared, "Holy shit!"

"Yeah, that's what I said the first time," Shane said with a wink as they clambered into the Jeep. "When you're handcuffed like that you're supposed to give your complete trust. But let me just warn ya: Ginger LaFond is not to be trusted. Not at all."

"Whoa."

* * * * *

Knowing that he could find Tom Jacobs on a bar stool, Mike pressed through the glass doors of the Post-Time Bar. The dimly lit lounge was tucked in a far corner of the racetrack. The surface of the bar was chipped and stained, as were the mismatched bowls that held the pretzels and nuts. A blue miasma of stale cigarette smoke wafted through the air. A close-circuit TV that featured the evening's races hung in the right corner of the bar. On the screen of the TV to the left was a group of retired football players dressed in Armani suites discussing the upcoming games. Like most of the bar's patrons, the light fixtures were outdated and dusty.

The Post-Time Bar was a place where horse-men hung out. It wasn't as upscale as the clubhouse where most of the racing fans gathered. Rather, it was a place where the agents watched the races while making deals with trainers and old jockeys traded yarns of the good ol' days.

Looking around the room, Mike spotted three old jockeys with cigarettes dangling from their weathered lips at a corner table. Sitting at the bar with a beer in his fist was Tom Jacobs. Mike nodded at the jockeys, gestured to the bartender for a beer, and then slid onto the barstool next to Tom.

"Tom..." Mike said, as the bartender delivered his beer.

The tip of Tom's cigar was like a red cannon ball in the dim lights. "Hey, Mike, how's my boy Dave workin' out?" he asked in his slow southern drawl.

Mike took a sip of his beer. "He's interesting. He seems awfully ... enlightened."

The cigar rotated around in Tom's lips while he studied Mike.

Mike continued, "For example, he knows what drugs this track is testing for and when. Any thoughts on where a newbie bug boy gets that kind of information?"

Taking away the empty glasses, the bartender delivered Tom another double shot of Jack.

The agent tugged the cigar from his mouth to stare at the lit end, and then he dragged his gaze to meet Mike's. "Ya know there're a lot of trainers makin' money on throwaway horses that only needed a little pick-me-up."

"Otherwise known as cheating," Mike quietly bit out.

Tom wrapped his stubby fingers around the shot glass and then threw the whiskey back. "Do yourself a favor, Mike. Back off."

Disgusted, Mike tossed several bills on the bar and slid from the stool.

Tom grabbed him by the arm. "Listen..."

Mike yanked his arm from Tom's grip. He turned to see Chip Walker leaning on the wall next to the door, gnawing on a toothpick. His two huge goons stood on the other side of the doorway.

Tom muttered, "You'd best be on your way, son."

Mike looked back at Tom. "Are you part of this, Jacobs?"

Tom smashed his cigar into an ashtray. "I just don't want to see a good customer get himself hurt, Mike."

"Pfft," was all that Mike could manage before heading to the door. "Mike..." Chip said, with a nod.

"Chip..."

The two men stared at each other for a moment, until Parker stepped into the doorway to block Mike's exit. The big man crossed his hefty arms across his expansive chest. His expression was impassive yet his body language screamed, *On Chip's word I'll beat you to a pulp.*

"You and your brother sure do like pokin' your noses around where they don't belong." Chip pulled the toothpick from his mouth and flicked it to the floor. "That's a good way to get your noses broke. Ain't that right, Parker?"

A wide smile slithered across the big thug's face. Saying nothing, he nodded his agreement as he examined his large calloused knuckles.

Mike was out-muscled.

"What are you? The Keystone Mafioso?" Mike inquired with a curt tone.

Chip threw back his head laughing. "Nah, nothing like that. We just don't want to see you get into trouble is all. You get my meaning? We'll all get along just fine if we stay out of each other's way. You understand?"

"More than you know." Mike said.

Chip's lips curled into a greasy grin. "Good." He nodded at Parker who stepped aside to give Mike exit. "Nice talkin' to ya, Mike. You take care now, ya hear?"

Disdain coil through Mike's gut. His glare rotated from Chip to Parker, and then knowing that it was in his best interest to shut-up, he shouldered past the brute out of the Post-Time Bar.

* * * * *

Barney's Bar and Grill was hopping. The parking lot was full. When Shane and Dave stepped inside, they noticed that every stool at the bar was occupied, and the pool tables were surrounded by a crowd three deep.

Shane scanned the mass of people. Then, with a grin on his handsome face, he elbowed Dave and hitched his chin toward a tiny brunette wearing a taunt tank top, a pair of riding breeches, and riding boots with a crop stuffed inside the left boot.

"There she is...Ginger LaFond," Shane said over the hum of the crowd. "Let's get some beers and I'll introduce you. She's wicked with that freakin' crop. So don't say you weren't warned."

Dave couldn't take his eyes off the girl while they made their way through the mob toward the bar.

Barney was a short tubby man, who wore his head shaved and a crisp white apron over his clothing. He caught a glimpse of Shane and called out, "Whatta ya having, West?"

"Two beers, Barney," Shane called back.

Two girls wiggled from their seats to make their way toward the pool tables. Shane and Dave grabbed the opportunity to have a seat. Barney delivered the beers.

"I've got these." Dave shoved money across the bar when a loud voice boomed behind them.

"Hey, Blake!"

Dave and Shane twisted on their stools to see who was making the ruckus.

Suddenly the bar grew very quiet.

A large disheveled-looking man pressed through the throng toward them. His face was flushed with anger and his hands were balled into fists at his side.

Having never seen this man before, Dave tossed Shane a questioning look.

Shane leaned close to Dave. "Stan Urick...badass with a big-ass temper."

"Not good," Dave replied.

"It's not looking that way."

Dave took a deep breath and a swig of his beer.

Stan hovered over them. He poked Dave in the shoulder, hard. "Weren't you ridin' Bishop's horse in the fifth race?"

Casually, Dave placed his beer on the bar. "I was. What about it?"

Stan's face twisted in agitation. "Mine was the five horse. You and that drug addict you were ridin' bumped into him and practically knocked him down! Cost me the fuckin' race!"

A small group of young women hurried out the door. Barney grabbed his baseball bat from under the bar.

Dave tried to remain calm. "Look, I'm sorry if I bumped your horse, but I don't think it cost you the race. If I remember correctly from the program, your horse went off at fifty to one."

"He was gonna run big tonight!" Stan bellowed.

"You should've lodged a complaint with the stewards. I can't help you," Dave said, clipped.

"I'm sick and tired of you drug usin' cheatin' bastards!" Stan grabbed Dave by the sleeve of his shirt.

Dave raised his hands. "Don't go there, dude."

Stan wasn't listening. He threw a punch. Dave ducked under Stan's arm and came up at his back with his fist raised and his feet planted far apart. Surprised to find the smaller man behind him, Stan whirled around. That's when Dave punched and jabbed like a pro.

The crowd scattered to the perimeter of the bar. Hooting and hollering, they yelled instructions to both men.

Awe struck at Dave's agility and crisp fighting technique, Shane watched from his bar stool.

Dancing from foot to foot, Dave blocked and ducked Stan's advances. Still, the large man managed to shove Dave against the bar.

Quickly, Shane took up the beers and hastened out of the way.

Barney tapped the bat on the bar. "Break it up, boys! I don't want to bust no one's balls!" he hollered to be heard over the crowd.

Pushing away from the bar before Stan could trap him, Dave hit the large man hard with an upper cut to the jaw. He then punched him in the gut.

Stan's head snapped sideways, and then he bent over from the strike to his stomach. Bowing his head, he attempted to head-butt Dave, who quickly stepped aside, allowing Stan to ram into the bar. He fell to his knees.

Barney smacked the bat on the bar again. "C'mon boys! Don't wreck the place! I'm gonna come out there!" he threatened from behind the security of the bar.

Stan grabbed a bar stool for leverage to stand. Blood gushed from his nose. Cheers and boos rose from the crowd as the big man swaggered toward Dave. He took another swipe at the slight built man like a grizzly bear trying to catch a tiny fish in the stream, but only managed to knock himself off balance and fall face first to the floor.

The crowd laughed.

Ginger LaFond had weaved her way through the crowd to where Shane was standing. "Who is that?" she hissed in Shane's ear.

"Dave Blake, he's a bug." Shane told her.

She pulled the crop from her boot. Smiling, she slapped the boot with it.

Shane asked, "Would you like an intro?"

"Mmm...it's a possibility."

Breathing heavily, Dave stood over Stan to see what he was going to do next.

Finally, Stan heaved his body from the floor. Gasping for air, he shook his finger at Dave and then stumbled out the door.

Cheers and laughter rang through the building.

Shane handed Dave his beer. "I think you can eliminate his stable from your list of possibilities."

"Ya think?" Dave lifted the beer to his lips and took a long drink.

"Let's get the hell out of here before he comes back with reinforcements," Shane suggested.

Dave chugged the rest of his beer, and made his way toward the door.

Holding the door open for Dave, Shane said, "Seriously dude, you should pick the stables you ride for more carefully. Where did you learn to fight like that?"

"I have four older sisters."

~ FIVE ~

The next morning, the rumors were flying throughout the backside of the track about the big fight that took place at Barney's between the bug boy, Dave Blake, and the horse trainer, Stan Urick. Events such as fights, affairs, or the combination were fodder for gossip in the small community that was Keystone Downs.

Because the gossip mill wasn't exactly the most reliable source of accurate information, Mike and Punch were sitting in the barn office absorbed in Shane's version of what actually went on at Barney's. Shane was more than enthusiastic to reiterate the incident.

"I couldn't believe my eyes," he was telling them. "Dave was dancin' around like Evander freakin' Holyfield."

Punch snorted. "So ol' Stan Urick was pretty bent, was he?"

"Oh, I thought Dave was gonna get his ass kicked into next Tuesday."

"And Dave just took Stan out?" Punch asked.

"Like right now, dude." Shane turned toward his older brother sitting at the desk with his legs propped up. Chewing on a sprig of straw, he was listening intently. Shane asked, "What do you think about that, bro?"

Mike shook his head. "I think we've got a bug boy that showed up out of nowhere with a big time agent, knows way too much about the track's drug testing procedures, no one knows anything about him, and he fights like a pro. You've gotta ask yourself: what's wrong with this picture? Is this some kind of set-up?"

"Are you still planning to have him exercise Sheldon at the track next week?" Punch asked.

"Yeah," Mike said, "as a matter of fact I may assign several more horses to Dave Blake. I want him where I can watch him."

"Sorry, Mike, I don't think so," a voice said from the doorway of the office.

They looked up to see Eric filling the doorway with Paul Young at his side. Mike dropped his feet from the desk. Eric said, "Boys, you remember Paul Young, our head steward here at the track."

Shaking hands with each, Paul explained, "Dave Blake has been put on three days suspension for fighting, effective immediately. Keystone simply can't tolerate violence like that from our bug boys or our jockeys. It's track policy."

Immediately, Shane came to Dave's defense. "I don't get it. The fight wasn't on track property, and Stan threw the first punch. Dave was only defending himself."

Paul explained, "And Stan Urick won't be racing any horses for the next three days either. He's been suspended as well."

Eric shot Shane a look that definitely screamed, back off. Offering the steward his hand, he turned to him. "Thanks for stopping by to let us know, Paul. We appreciate it."

Paul shook his hand, "It was on my way out. Sorry, boys, take care now."

Eric walked him out of the barn.

Spinning his chair toward Punch and Shane, Mike warned, "I'm tellin' ya, something's about to blow."

* * * * *

A crisp breeze swept through the shed rows. The very edge of autumn was in the air. It was Kate's favorite time of the year. She loved to watch the trees turn hues of yellow and orange, and then fall gently to the ground as summer bid her farewell with the promise of return. Kate couldn't bear to shut out autumn by closing the office door. So she left it wide open. Holden had offered to pick up lunch from the cafeteria while she set up the desk for them to eat at.

She had just set out the forks and napkins on the placemats when an unwelcome voice called to her, "Hello, Angel, what's for lunch?"

Kate's head jerked up to find Chip filling the doorway. The backsplash of light allowed for only his silhouette, except she recognized his voice. When he stepped into the room, the smile on his face and his wandering eyes instantly made her feel violated.

The women who worked the backside of Keystone downs—stable hands, exercise riders, and even the female jockeys— Chip Walker breathtaking. They flirted and threw themselves at him shamelessly. Kate surmised that it was his creamy caramel skin, or perhaps his thick dark wavy hair that had the women in a tailspin. Although he was not as tall as Kate's fiancé or her overtly handsome brothers, Chip had a well-toned physique. Regardless of his skin hair or body form, Chip Walker had no affect on Kate whatsoever. She considered him the type of man that would lure a woman into his bedroom and then treat her like garbage afterward.

Kate regarded him in an extremely very business-like manner. "What can I do for you, Chip?"

He crossed the room to lay his hands on the desk and leaned toward her. "I just stopped by to see if your boyfriend has any DMSO."

Kate held her ground. Her nostrils flared. "I'm sure he does," she replied. "However, I can't give it to you without his consent."

Chip licked his lips like a lion licking his chops. Stepping away from the desk, he flopped into the metal chair. "Gotta have it. Mind if I wait for him? Nice office, I mean with you in it." Stretching out his legs out and crossing one ankle over the other, he looked at her like she was a piece of meat to be devoured.

"Suit yourself."

"I'm suited just fine, thank you. I see Mike's got Shady Deal in the sixth race tonight. Wonder if Quaide will claim him back. I know his panties have been in a bunch ever since Westwood took him."

Kate crossed her arms under her breasts. "Westwood didn't take him. They claimed him."

Shrugging, he enjoyed the slight flush in her cheeks and the bite in her eyes. "Same thing."

"I think not."

"What do you want, Chip?" Holden's terse voice rang through the small space.

Chip didn't look up. His grin stretched up to his brown eyes. "I just stopped by for a bottle of DMSO, but your lovely assistant slash girlfriend said she couldn't give me none without your say-so." He turned to face Holden. "Ain't that ironic?"

Holden glared at him. He carried the take-out bags into the office and set them on the desk in front of Kate. Purposefully, he crossed the room to the shelving units to retrieve a bottle of DMSO, which he dropped into Chip's lap.

Flinching, Chip lifted it from his crotch. With a grunt, he muttered, "Thanks."

"I'll send a bill for that," Kate quickly put in.

"You do that, Angel." With that, he pushed from the chair to saunter to the door. Holden followed him out and closed the door behind them.

"What are you doing at my office?" Holden demanded.

"I was counting the hairs on her pretty little head. You missed two texts this morning."

"I'm a veterinarian. I'm busy. Now get the fuck out of here, and don't come back."

"Whatever you say, Doc."

* * * * *

"Whoa, big guy," Shane whispered to the immense gelding, Shady Deal, while Mike knelt next to him to tighten an ice boot to his right front leg.

The boots were made of thick material with pockets filled with ice to increase blood circulation to keep down inflammation from which the horse may suffer.

After Mike smoothed the Velcro straps down tautly, and then he secured another pair of ice boots to the left leg Shady fussed and pawed in the straw with his right hoof.

Standing, Mike patted the gelding's shoulder. "That's good. Easy now."

Checking his watch, Eric said, "We've got about an hour before they call us to the paddock. Let's go to the cafeteria and get some burgers."

"Sounds good." Shane unlatched the lead from Shady Deal's halter. Mike held the stall gate open until Shane stepped into the aisle.

With an ornery grin, Shane asked his father, "Are you sure you shouldn't call Jen and see if you're allowed to have a burger from the cafeteria? I've heard her complain that they're full of grease and fat."

Mike chuckled at Shane's good-natured needling.

"What Jen doesn't know won't hurt her," Eric said.

Shane winked at Mike. "Yeah, but if she asks me, I'll have to tell her the truth. I'm just sayin'..."

"Don't make me kill you, Shane." Eric held the barn door open for his sons to step through. Their goading at his girlfriend's protective nature urged a smile from him. If his boys didn't like Jen, they wouldn't be teasing him. It felt good to know he had their unspoken approval and that Jen had their love. He turned off the aisle lights before following them out and leaving the barn dimly lit with only the stall lights left burning.

The horses settled into eating their hay. The soft drone of the barn radio was like a lullaby.

Shady Deal nibbled at the Velcro straps on his ice boots. His lips flapped at them. He ran his teeth up and down while looking for a loose piece of Velcro to yank, except Mike had smoothed them down firmly. The gelding shook his head and snorted at the boots while stomping his hooves in the straw.

A slice of light swept down the barn aisle when the door opened. The silhouette of a large man filled the doorway. The horses looked up from their munching.

Shady Deal hesitated from his task.

The dark shadow eased the door closed. A slight beam from a flashlight gleamed while he slowly made his way down the aisle. He stopped to peer into stalls and shone the light in horse's faces. They would duck away to the back of their stalls from the intrusive ray. His footsteps were slow and measured.

Finally, he came to Shady Deal's stall. Shining the flashlight in on the gelding, he took note of the ice boots on his front legs. It was a pre-race preparation that many trainers used—the ice boots were a signal that this horse was about to be taken to the racing paddock.

"Mmmm," he murmured from deep in his throat. He turned off the flashlight. The stall light was satisfactory. He unlatched the gate and stepped into the stall with Shady Deal.

* * * * *

Holden rolled the vet truck to a stop in front of Westwood Stables. "Don't take too long, Kate. We don't want to fall behind or we won't get back to my apartment until after midnight."

"Aw, will the sexy cowboy be too tired for the sassy cowgirl?" Kate teased.

The right side of his lips curled into an ornery grin. He poked her in the ribs. "I'm never too tired, baby."

"Ain't it the truth? I'll be right back. I just want to wish them luck with Shady Deal tonight." Kate jumped from the truck and trotted to the stable door. When she pressed through, she switched on the main lights. The horses whinnied, and whirled in their stalls. Peeking over their gates, they shook their heads at her with wide eyes and flared nostrils.

Finding the horses so fussed-up odd; she cocked her head to the side and narrowed her eyes. She made her way down the aisle toward the barn office, while calling out, "Dad...Mike...are you in here?" She came to a stop as if someone had tossed a bucket of water over her when she saw a pool of blood at the threshold of Shady Deal's stall.

The gate hung open. The metal rungs dripped with a thick coating of blood. Taking a step back, Kate gasped and drew her hand to her mouth. She approached the stall with hesitation in each step. As she drew closer her eyes fell upon the blood soaked straw lying in the stall.

On a braced breath she stepped through the gate. "Oh my God!"

Shady Deal swaggered back and forth. His head hung below his chest with his scalp cracked open. Blood spewed down his chest and his legs filling the ice boots. His forelock was caked in thick clots and the blood was spattered over his withers.

"Holden!" Kate screamed while spinning on her heels to dash down the aisle to the door. "Holden!" She flung the barn door open. Holden was jumping from the truck.

"What's wrong, Kate?" He grabbed her by the shoulders.

Kate shook with fear. Unable to form words, she pointed toward the stall.

Holden's eyes widened and his jaw dropped at the sight of the blood. "Is the horse dead?"

Kate's mouth was dry and tight, she could barely respond. She shook her head no.

"Get the vet box from the truck. Hurry!" He dashed down the aisle to the stall.

Darting out of the stable, Kate bumped into her father.

"Whoa slow down, what's your hurry?" Eric caught his daughter in his arms.

Kate swallowed hard.

Standing behind their father, Mike and Shane could see the angst in her face.

Eric inquired, "What's wrong, Kate?"

Her voice came out in short hiccups. "Someone beat Shady Deal! I have to get the vet box!" She pushed past them to run to the truck.

Eric, Mike, and Shane hurried through the door and down the aisle. Each came to a shocking halt when they saw Holden in the stall. Holding up the head of a mangled Shady Deal, Holden yanked on the straps of the ice boots.

"What the hell happened?" Mike demanded to know.

"I don't know! We found him like this," Holden tossed the bloody ice boots into a corner before shaking the blood from his hands.

Kate pushed through her brothers and her father to hand off the vet box to Holden. She dumped a bundle of gauze into a stainless steel bucket that she'd filled with water. Holden quickly opened the box and handed her a bottle of Betadine Surgical Scrub. She squeezed the solution into the water and over the gauze to turn everything in the bucket and the gauze orange. Then, she grabbed the gauze and proceeded to wash Shady Deal's gaping wounds.

Holden stood out of the way while she prepped the horse for his examination. His stomach was a tight twist of knots. The conversation he had had with Chip outside this very stable only a few days earlier haunted him: "Don't follow me to the West's stable. I don't want them to think that we're friends. They're getting more suspicious every day." He remembered telling Chip.

"Don't worry. The Wests will back off. You'll see." Chip said.

He recalled grabbing Chip by the T-shirt, demanding, "What the hell is that supposed to mean?"

Chip brushed his hand away. He stated, "Do what you're told, Doc. I'll take care of the rest."

Good God. Is this what Chip had in mind? Was this not only a warning to the Wests, but to him as well? The short amount of time that he had to examine Shady Deal, he could tell that the injuries had been from blunt force trauma with an object such as a bat—maybe a baseball bat, or perhaps a two by four. With the amount of damage that had been done to the animal—a very large animal—it had to be with a great amount of force. The kind of force that a big man could wield—like one of Chip's thugs, and then he remembered a big man stepping into Chip's barn the other day during another tight conversation. Chip told him, "That's Parker. His job is to make sure that he always knows where Miss

Kate West is. You know, just in case your cooperation level would take a dip, and I haven't been very happy with the way you've been ignoring my calls and texts."

Oh yeah, Parker was a brute. He had mean eyes and plenty of bulk to wield. Holden winced at the thought of what Chip and his cronies were capable of. Kate was almost finished cleaning the wound. He would be able to finish his examination and then begin to stitch the horse back together. From the looks of it, Shady Deal practically needed his face stitched back on and his head closed up. He was hopeful that the horse could make a full recovery, but he was certain that Shady Deal would never be the same.

"Holden..." He flinched when he heard Mike's voice. When he made eye contact, he realized that Mike had been trying to get his attention for some time.

"I'm sorry...what?"

"I asked if there is anything that we can do?" Mike repeated.

"Stay out of the way," he said tersely, "let me do my job."

"I think we're ready." Kate tried to steady the horse that was staggering trying to stay on his feet.

"Everyone out of the stall," Holden instructed, "I'm going to lay him down to work on him." The

West men stepped into the aisle. Holden rolled the main stall door closed.

Eric sunk onto a bale of straw and dropped his elbows onto his knees. He looked at the floor between his boots without really seeing it.

Folding his arms over his chest, Mike leaned against the wall. "I think someone just sent us a message."

"Dan Quaide was pretty pissed off at the party," Shane recalled.

"No, this is too obvious, even for Quaide," Eric said.

"Chip Walker wasn't too thrilled when he saw me questioning Tom Jacobs at the bar the other night," Mike said. "He let me know in no uncertain terms that he didn't like us poking around, and that we should mind our own business."

Shane pushed from the wall he was leaning on. "He said the same to me the other day. Maybe we should question Chip Walker." He bolted toward the door.

Eric caught him by the arm. "Put a lid on it. We need to keep cool. Let's talk around the track. Surely, someone saw a person or a vehicle around our barn about a half-hour ago." He hitched his chin in Mike's direction. "Go trackside see what you can find out. Shane, talk to the pony-riders. They always see and hear things on their way to and from the paddock. I'm going to see Paul Young to let them know that Shady Deal won't make it to the post parade tonight." With a warning, he rose from the bale. "Keep alert. If they're capable of doing this to a horse, they won't have any qualms about beating on a human being."

* * * * *

"Michael..." Ava called from the coffee stand located next to the door that led to the grandstands.

Mike turned to find his beautiful auburn-haired ex-wife coming toward him with two coffees in hand. "Hey, Ava, what's up?"

"I heard what happened to your horse," she said. "I'm sorry."

"Wow, I know news travels fast around here, but that's just ridiculous."

"Doc got a call from the stewards," she explained. "They said Eric was in their office. He came right over to see if there was anything that he could do. We'll probably pick up as many of Holden's stops as possible tonight, so I came here to fill our travel mugs."

"Holden's going to be busy trying to put Shady Deal back together for a few hours. It's pretty bad. I'm here to see if anyone saw or heard anything suspicious around our barn tonight."

Ava bit her lip. Her gaze dropped to the travel mugs in her hands. Mike knew that look. Ava was holding something back.

"What's wrong, Ava?" he asked. "Did you see something?" She let out a breath. Closing the distance between them, he softened his tone to a whisper. "Talk to me, Avie."

Slowly, she dragged her gaze to meet his. He had the most incredible hazel eyes. She loved Mike's eyes: so beautiful, so intense and probing. Glancing around for unwelcome eavesdroppers, she lowered her voice. "I'm not sure. Doc Spears has been keeping a close eye on Chip Walker for quite some time. He thinks he's up to no good. Doc believes he's connected to a drug ring here at the track."

"You're not tellin me anything that I'm surprised by, Ava."

"Probably not, but guess who we saw arguing with Chip the other day ... *Holden.*"

Mike's eyes narrowed, his nostrils flared.

"The argument was pretty intense," she continued. "We see Holden's truck parked at Chip's stable a lot. Kate is never with him. I'm not surprised. When I was Holden's assistant we stopped there all the time, but I was never allowed to get out of the truck. When Holden would come out of Chip's stable he would be mean and nasty—like someone I'd never met before. Something's going on between Chip and Holden, and it isn't good."

Mike's jaw clenched. Could he believe her? Or was this one of Ava's manipulative maneuvers that she'd conjured up because of the history she had with Holden? Was this some kind of attempt to hurt Kate? His five-year marriage to Ava had proved one thing: the woman was capable of diabolical lies.

Suddenly, he felt the warmth of her hand against his skin. She wrapped her fingers around his wrist and squeezed. His hazel eyes looked into her green bedroom eyes, except they weren't in seduction mode. They were filled with a different purpose. Ava whispered, "I wouldn't lie about something this important, Michael."

He could see the sincerity bleeding from her expression. "I hope not, Ava. I'm going to look into it." He turned to walk away.

Ava held onto his wrist.

He looked back at her.

"Be careful, Michael," she said. "I truly believe that Chip Walker is a very dangerous man."

He believed her.

CINDY MCDONALD

PART TWO

SHADES OF DARKNESS

~ SIX ~

Scrubbing his fingers over his five-o'clock shadow that was more like a nine o'clock beard, Lieutenant Carl Lugowski had just finished his report, turned it into his captain, and was about to grab his jacket from the back of his chair, when his cell phone rang. He looked at the caller ID: Ava West. Smiling, he lifted the phone to his ear. "Hey, baby, what's going on?"

Ava's voice was filled with bother. She whispered, "I'm really scared, Carl. Something awful is going on at the track. Someone beat one of Michael's horses half to death. I told you about the argument that Doc and I saw between Chip Walker and Holden Reese. I don't know what to think, but I've got a real bad feeling about all of it."

Shrugging into his jacket, Lugowski asked, "You're worried about your ex? That's new. Did Mike do something to piss Walker off?"

"It doesn't matter, Carl. People don't go into stables and beat horses with two by fours. If someone had attacked Michael, I'd be upset, but it would make more sense. It would be more direct. This has a mob-like warning written all over it. I'm almost surprised that he didn't find the horse's head in the back of his pickup truck."

"Whoa, you think this Walker is Godfather dangerous?"

"I do."

Lugowski sank into the chair at his desk. He didn't like the sound of that. Moreover, he didn't like the trepidation in Ava's voice. "Let me do some checking," he said. "In the meantime, stay out of harm's way. Stick close to Doc Spears, okay?"

"Okay." With that, Ava hung up.

Lugowski leaned back against the chair. Oh well, so much for going to his apartment and that hot shower that he was looking forward to. Pushing from his seat, he made his way across the homicide unit into the hallway. He knew exactly where to get the information he needed. He trotted up the old dusty stairwell to the next floor which housed the gang and drug unit where he was certain he would find Jack Haliday.

Sure enough, he spotted the ex-Navy SEAL tapping at the computer on his desk. His jacket was slung over his chair and the blue hue from the computer's screen illuminated the five o'clock shadow that he was sporting and his very dark hair. Steam curled into the air above his coffee cup resting among the piles of paperwork.

Lugowski went over to his desk, plopped down in the chair that was positioned next to it, snatched the cup from his desk, and took a big drink. He made a gagging sound. "What's the matter with you gang buster boys? Sugar makes you too sweet?" Wincing, he put the cup back on Jack's desk.

Without flinching or taking his eyes off the computer's screen, Jack said, "It would take a whole pound of sugar to sweeten me up. What brings you up to my lowly end of the precinct, Lugowski? Murder and mutilation starting to bore you?"

Lugowski snorted, "Something like that. I got a phone call from my girlfriend, Ava West. She said that Mike West had one of his horses beaten almost to death at the track tonight. She's worried that it was a warning from a mob within the track."

Jack leaned back in his seat and crossed his arms over his wide chest. "Suddenly," Lugowski continued, "I'm remembering a conversation that you and I had some months back. You said that you were watching Dr. Holden Reese. Do you have a man inside the track watching a trainer by the name of Chip Walker, too?"

Jack picked up his coffee and took a sip. "Ahhh, just right." He measured Lugowski for a moment. "We brought a man in from the Philadelphia gang unit. He's posing as a jockey. Our unit didn't have anyone small enough to do the assignment." Jack spread his arms out wide. "I'm hardly jockey material."

He was right. Jack was six foot two of solid muscle that weighed in at about one-ninety-five.

"We were tipped-off a few months ago that a drug ring was operating at the track. It took us a while to get our man trained up for the task, but he's in there right now infiltrating the trainers and jockeys. He said he'd check in at the end of the week. I should be hearing from him tonight. I'll let you know if he's got anything."

"Thanks," Lugowski said.

"We checked out your girlfriend, since she used to work for Dr. Reese. She was clean."

"I know," Lugowski said. "For that matter, you won't find any dirt on the Wests."

Jack smiled. "Still got it bad for that pretty blonde? What's her name? Kate."

"Up your ass, Haliday, I've got a girl."

Turning back to his computer screen, Jack muttered, "Yeah, yeah, yeah."

Lugowski made his way to the parking lot. There was no way he could go home now. He needed to go to the track to check on Ava. Maybe he should check on the Wests, as well.

It wasn't his investigation. Still, making sure that everyone was okay couldn't hurt.

Kate would be upset over the incident.

Wait a minute...that wasn't any of his business, right?

*****

Ripping his tie from his collar and tossing it onto the passenger's seat, Lugowski flashed his badge at the security guard at the stable gate at Keystone Downs. The guard inside the shack nodded and pressed a button. The old metal gate with peeling yellow paint groaned as it opened to give the unmarked police SUV access to the stable area, otherwise known as "the backside" of the track. Lugowski drove through the shed rows in search of Doc Spears' vet truck when he spotted Kate digging through the drawers of the vet compartment in the backend of Holden's truck.

He slowed the SUV to a stop and slid from his seat. "How's the horse, Kate?"

Turning, Kate favored him with a weary smile. Though she was tired, her blue eyes mesmerized him. She was beautiful in the daylight, and she was breathtaking in the dim lighting of the evening.

Kate West was what Lugowski considered a "keeper." The kind of woman to come home to after a long day, make love to all night, and cherish to your dying day. But she was Holden Reese's keeper, not his.

"He's not good, and he'll never be the same." She let out a fatigued breath. "But he's alive and will make a recovery. Holden's not sure how much of one, yet."

He could see that this terrible incident had shaken her to the core. He didn't blame her. Moreover, he had to fight the urge to take her into his arms and comfort her. Damn, he always had to fight such urges when Kate West was present. The woman set off all his primal desires on sight. He couldn't understand it, and it scared the hell out of him.

He swallowed hard. "Have you called the police?"

"The track authorities are aware of the situation, but I don't know that the police will be involved. It's...complicated, Carl."

He dragged his gaze away from her eyes down to his feet out of shame. He could feel the thump of an erection beginning to grow. Damn it, what the hell's wrong with you, Lugowski?

He blurted out. "I'd better be going. I just wanted to check in."

"Thank you for that, Carl. You're a good friend."

He managed a svelte smile and then made his way back to the SUV. Kate watched him drive down the shed row. Each time she bumped into Carl Lugowski, she found herself wondering about his relationship with her ex-sister-in-law, Ava. He really was a catch. If she hadn't been with Holden she may have very well considered the lieutenant romantically, if he could let go of that green-eyed manipulative monstrosity that he called his girlfriend. Shaking those thoughts from her head, she turned back to the medical supplies and the task at hand: Shady Deal.

~ SEVEN ~

With the races almost over for the night, many of the stables were dark. The dusk-to-dawn lights lent a hazy glow throughout the shed rows. Watching the cats dart through the shadows in search for rats, the pigeons had settled into their nests on the tin roofs. The steam rose from the manure bins like phantoms being released into the night.

It had taken several hours to stabilize and stitch up Shady Deal. Holden took extra care and time about bringing him to consciousness and to his feet. After a long discussion, and making sure that the horse was able to stand, it was decided to load Shady Deal onto a horse trailer and haul him to the farm where they could keep a close eye on him.

Mike removed the stall divides from the inside of the horse trailer and covered the floor with thick layers of straw before parking it in front of Westwood

Stables. Kate led Shady Deal slowly down the aisle, while the men lined up alongside: Mike and Shane on the horse's right side, while Eric and Holden took up the left to ensure the horse's balance when he walked up the ramp into the trailer.

Eric and Mike climbed into the truck.

Shane went to the driver's side window where his brother was preparing for the very slow and cautious drive home. "I'll close up the barn for the night. Take it easy on the way home, bro."

Leaning forward so he could see Shane past Mike, Eric asked, "Are you coming straight home afterward?" He was concerned that Shady Deal wouldn't be the only target tonight.

Shane chuckled to himself. "I think I'm going to stop in at the Post Time Bar for a beer. After the riders have had a few, tongues could loosen up. I might find something out."

"Not a bad idea." Eric pointed a finger across Mike's chest at his youngest and cautioned him. "Be careful." Nodding in agreement, Mike eased the truck forward to roll slowly through the shed rows toward the security gate. After they safely turned the corner, Shane returned to the stable to clean up.

He grabbed a wheelbarrow that was leaning against the wall and a pitchfork. Parking it at the door of the stall, Shane pitched the bloodied straw into the wheelbarrow and disposed of the blood-stained ice boots into a garbage can. He dumped the wheelbarrow into one of the manure bins positioned in the middle of the roadway between the shed rows before returning to do a general clean up of the stable. When he heard the barn door creak open, Shane froze. Listening to the footsteps making their way through the stable, he took hold of the pitchfork as if it were a baseball bat, and waited.

"Hello...anyone here?" he heard Dave Blake's voice call out.

Letting out a relieved breath, Shane stepped out of Shady Deal's stall. Dave was dressed in a pair of jeans, a jacket, and a pair of Nikes. Because of his suspension, he wasn't wearing the usual riding attire.

"Hey Shane...I heard what happened. How's Shady?"

"Not too good. They beat the hell out of him."

"Any idea who did it?"

Shane liked Dave but not knowing him well enough, he wasn't ready to share suspicions with him. "Nope. I was just about to get a beer at the Post Time. Wanna come?"

"Um, I've got something to do first. I'll meet you there in twenty minutes or so."

Casting the last bit of clean straw over the stall floor, Shane said, "Good enough."

Dave made his way back through the stable. Hearing him open and close the barn door, Shane followed. What could a suspended rider have to do at the track this late in the evening? At this point in the game, everyone was suspect, especially newcomers.

Dave stepped out of Westwood Stables into the shed rows that were mostly quiet and abandoned for the night. Making his way along the stables, he could hear the clip clop of horses trotting over the pavement one row down and the laughter of pony riders leading the last group of Thoroughbreds from the races back to their stables.

He dipped into the shadows in order to not to be seen by anyone. When the voices and sound of hooves faded into the distance, he scurried across the roadway to the next line of shed rows. Keeping close to the buildings, he crept along furtively until Walker Stables came into view. The stable was dark and closed up for the night. Although rooms inside the stables were most likely locked, tack rooms, feed rooms, and barn offices, the stable doors were never locked so that animals could be removed by anyone in case of an emergency, such as a fire.

Dave scanned the shed row and the roadway to make sure no one was around. Ducking low, he jogged past the ornate wrought iron bracket that held a sign that read: Walker Stables. He made his way to the stable door and slid into the barn.

The aisle was clean swept. Bales of straw and hay were neatly piled along the wall across from the stalls. Likewise, wheelbarrows, pitchforks, and brooms were lined up against the wall. The radio had been turned down to low for the night. Yet a heavy beat of rap music pulsed through the speakers.

The horses peeked from their stalls at the stranger holding a small flashlight in the doorway.

Dave shot the beams up and down the aisle until it settled on a door with a deadbolt. Figuring that the locked door must lead to Chip's office, he made his way toward the door when a voice from behind him whispered, "What're you doin'?"

Dave flinched. He whipped around to find Shane squinting and shielding his eyes from the beam of his flashlight.

"Shane..."

"I don't think anyone's here. Chip didn't have any horses racing tonight." Dave could hear the suspicion in Shane's voice.

"I know...but I left my crop here and I want to get it before I forget."

Shifting from one foot to the other, Shane furtively looked around the barn. "I think you should come back when Chip's here. He might have it locked in his office. C'mon, let's go get that beer."

"I'm just going to look around for it a little. You go ahead. I'll catch up with ya."

What is his deal? Shane thought. With a shrug of his shoulder and a lift of his eyebrow, he stepped out of the stable.

Dave didn't have much time. Furthermore, he realized that he just flew right into Shane's radar. He hurried to the locked door. Opening his jacket, he pulled a small lock pick from the inside pocket. He looked over his shoulder one more time.

The horses had dismissed him as a non-threat and returned to eating their hay. Satisfied with the stillness of the barn, he set to picking the lock until he heard a click. The corners of his mouth lifted at his achievement. He twisted the knob and slid through the door.

He hadn't been at Keystone Downs for long, but in that short period he had been in many of the barn offices to talk with trainers. The offices were a bare minimum—primitive. Even prestigious stables, such as Westwood, kept their office on the rugged side.

Chip's office was grand in comparison. The walls were covered in fine cherry paneling rather than the rough-cut pine like the others. Pictures of his racing victories were hung in perfect straight rows in ornate gold frames. His desk wasn't metal or old scarred wood. It was a sophisticated black lacquer desk that gleamed under the beams of his light. A floral throw rug lay across the floor. It looked like it had been purchased at a Walmart store.

Nonetheless, Chip had a rug rather than just a wood or dirt floor. It was so arrogant that it seemed out of place.

Dave set his beams on the wood shelving units that looked more like book shelves and began to pick up bottles and jars to examine the contents. Finally, he decided to look inside the desk only to find the drawers were locked.

Chip took the time to put a solid deadbolt on the door, and he locked the drawers to his very expensive desk.

Dave put his tiny lock picking tool to work again.

"What the hell are you doing, Dave?" Shane demanded from behind him.

Dave jumped and then let out an agitated breath. "Get out of here!"

"What are you looking for? If Walker finds us in here, he'll freak!"

"Then get out." Dave said.

With one more tweak, the lock clicked and the drawer slid open. Shining the flashlight into the drawer, Dave shuffled through papers and picked up a handful of slips to examine them.

Stepping in closer, Shane looked over Dave's shoulder. His eyes narrowed. "What did you find?"

"Prescriptions." Dave fingered through them.

"Seriously? For what?"

Steadying the flashlight on the slips, Dave replied, "You name it: Viagra, Procrit..."

"Who's writing them?"

"Your local drug pusher, Dr. Holden Reese."

"There's no way."

"Reese has been writing prescriptions for Walker," Dave explained. "He sells the drugs to the trainers, Walker kicks back to Reese, and presto! More stamina for the horses, more purse money for all."

"Not Holden. There's gotta be a mistake. Maybe the drugs are for Chip. Maybe he's got a problem getting it up."

"Wow, he's got a real problem. These dosages are for ten times what a human would require. There's got to be a pharmacist somewhere who's involved, too."

Shane snatched one of the slips from Dave's hand along with the flashlight. His face twisted when he read Holden's name on the slip.

"We've been watching this track for a while now," Dave said. "Dr. Spears has been our tip-off man."

"Who the hell are you?"

"Guess there's no point in hiding it now. I'm with the gang and drug unit in Philadelphia. I was brought in to infiltrate and gather intel on the illegal drugging of the horses at this track."

A nanosecond later the room was flooded with light. Chip filled the doorway, flanked by Ramon and Parker armed with guns that were fitted with silencers trained on the intruders.

Chip growled, "You Wests just can't take a hint, can you?"

"Whoa, Chip, it's just a couple of prescriptions," Shane said.

"It's Doc Reese's career and a whole lotta trainers losing a whole lotta money," Chip bit out. He snatched the prescriptions from Shane's hands and gathered the remaining slips that were in the drawer. Dropping them into a waste can next to the desk, he retrieved a lighter from his pocket and then lit them on fire.

Dave lunged forward burying his shoulder into Chip's stomach knocking him backward into Ramon and Parker. Chip fell to the floor. The two huge thugs lost their balance, but quickly recovered.

Shane kicked Ramon's right wrist which held the gun, but the brute held on tight. He whacked Shane across the jaw with the gun to throw him backward into the shelving unit. Bottles, jars, packages of bandages, and small equipment crashed to the floor on top of Shane while he scrambled to get to his feet. Ramon grabbed him by his shirt and punched him again to send Shane back to the floor before greeting him with the barrel of his gun to his forehead.

He flashed him a speaking look that screamed, *Go ahead, and give me a reason to pull the trigger.*

With no options left, Shane eased away while wiping the blood from his mouth.

Dave shuffled to escape the hold that Chip had on his clothing. He managed a quick jab to Chip's jaw to knock him further out the door, except when Dave clambered to his feet he heard a quick sputter like the venomous spit of a python, and then the burn and the pain in his shoulder that forced him to his knees.

Parker had shot him, and he had hit bone. Blood spewed through his clothing and the blazing pain shot through him like a scorching branding iron.

The sight of Dave's shattered shoulder brought Shane to his knees. He scrambled quickly on his hands and knees across the floor when Dave collapsed. "Holy shit!" Shane cried, "Give me something to press over this!"

Parker pulled Chip from the floor. Agitated and out of breath, Chip stated, "What the hell for? We're gonna kill you anyway."

Holding what was left of his shoulder, Dave lay on the floor. His chest pumped up and down in panic and pain. He was going into shock. Shane shrugged out of his jacket. He ripped the sleeve of his shirt, scrunched it into a ball and pressed it against the hole in Dave's shoulder. Then, he flung his jacket over Dave's torso.

Ramon turned to Chip. "What now? Parker just shot a freakin' cop."

"Take their cell phones," Chip instructed.

Ramon rifled through Shane's pockets and tossed his cell phone to Chip. Then, he did the same to Dave. Chip pitched the phones to the floor and stomped on them until they looked like mangled bits of nothing.

Chip said to Ramon, "Keep the lights off. Do everything by flashlight. Go into the empty stall at the end of the stable, dig a pit. You..." He turned to Parker, "Don't let either one of them move, if they do...use your imagination." With that, Chip turned toward the door.

"Where the hell are you going?" Ramon asked with a tug of panic in his tone. "We ain't handlin' this on our own, Chip."

"I'm going to find our loose end...Doc Spears," Chip hitched his chin toward the aisle where Ramon could find a shovel, and then he slipped out the barn door. He crept along the barn amongst the shadows until he rounded the corner out of sight. He flinched at the sound of horse's hooves clopping on the pavement coming in his direction. He sucked his body tightly against the wall.

Leading a sweaty Thoroughbred through the shed row, a young pony girl rode past him when she noticed a small ray of light from under the stable door at Walker Stables. She pulled her pony to a stop. Her eyes narrowed while she watched the beam disappear. Shrugging, she urged the pony forward to get the weary racehorse back to his stable.

~ EIGHT ~

Stan Urick was frustrated beyond composure. He marched back and forth across the doorway of the stall. Kate held on to a sorrel mare's lead, while Holden examined the horse's hind quarter. The hour had grown very late while Holden worked to care for Shady Deal. Doc Spears had covered quite a few of Holden's after-race rounds, but there were a few he couldn't get to.

Holden tried to concentrate on the mare, rather than Stan's yammering. "I just can't compete against those guys. I mean, they got those nags all pumped-up on stuff. You know what I mean, Doc?"

Irritation skittered down Holden's neck. "What are you bitchin' about, Stan? You're not even supposed to be running horses. Aren't you on three days suspension?"

Stan waved a careless hand at the vet. "No worries, I got Dan Quaide to run the horse for me tonight."

"Isn't that nice?" Kate put in. "The bug boy has to serve his days on suspension, but you've found a way around yours."

"Yeah, the world's a tough place, sweetheart," Stan said. "Ya know, Doc, I wouldn't mind gettin' in on that program...ya understand?"

Holden glanced quickly at Kate, who was wearing a baffled expression.

Stan continued to wheedle, "Then again, I'm afraid of gettin' caught, if you know what I mean."

The flush of irritation had settled on Holden's cheeks. He wanted Stan to shut-up. "Yeah, yeah, I know what you mean, Stan!" he snapped.

Kate flinched at his outburst.

Then, Holden's cell phone rang. "Gee-zuz! What now?" He looked at the screen: Chip Walker. "Great! Just what I need!" Stomping out of the stall, he put the phone to his ear. "What the hell do you want?"

"We've got a problem, Doc," Chip said. "Your girlfriend's brother has been hanging around with a cop that has been playing jockey. His name is Dave Blake. I found both of them in my office tonight poking around."

Holden continued to walk away from the stall to get out of Kate and Stan's earshot. His irritation was now mixing it up fast with panic. "Did they find anything?"

"The mother lode. Parker shot the cop, and now we've got a situation."

"Christ, Chip! What the hell are we going to do?"

"Ramon's digging a hole in a stall right now. We're gonna kill the bastards, put them in the hole, cover it with stall mats and straw, and then put a horse in there. No one will ever know what happened to Shane West and Dave Blake."

Holden fell against the barn wall. Beads of sweat dotted his forehead. He could barely catch his breath. He felt like the world was collapsing on top of him. "That's Kate's brother! I won't be a part of this! No way, Chip! You go straight to hell!" He thumbed the END button hard and shoved the phone back into his pocket.

Raking a harried hand through his hair, he felt like the oxygen had been sucked out of the atmosphere. He was going to lose everything. The beads of sweat where now dripping down his face in a steady stream. Swiping the sweat from stinging his eyes, he began to pace the aisle.

Kate called to him, "Holden, what's wrong?"

He spun on his heels. Trying to muster some poise, he swallowed a thick slug of salvia. His lips trembled while he tried to calm his voice. "Um...I've been called out of town...for...on business."

"What kind of business?" she asked.

Stan stepped out of the stall to see what the hold up was.

Holden's lips were dry like he'd been lying out in the Sahara Desert for days. He licked them. "A job. Like I told you, I want us to get out of here, Kate. So I applied for a vet position at...Lone Star Racetrack in Texas. What do you think?"

Kate's eyes narrowed. She could see the anxiety etched on Holden's face. Hesitantly, she said, "Wow, that's so far away. I'd have to think about it, Holden."

He rushed toward her and grabbed her by her shoulders. His fingers squeezed into her so hard that she thought he would break the skin. He spoke quickly and concise, "No, Kate, don't think. Just react. I love you, and I want you to be with me always. But I need to get away from here for a while. There's just too many people in our business—too many people in our way." He swallowed her into his chest. "Don't say no. Come with me, Baby."

"Well...of course I'd come with you, after you secure the job and after we get married. Then I could join you in Texas and we could begin our life together. If...if you're absolutely certain that's what you want. To be in Texas, I mean."

Holden took in a steadying breath. He let go of Kate to wipe his sweating palms down the sides of his jeans. He gave her a weak smile. "You're not getting it, Kate. I want you to come now. Right now.

Tonight. I can't do this alone. I need you with me. I need to know that you're on my side, no matter what. C'mon Kate, you're on my side, right?" He ran his fingers across her chin, down her neck, and squeezed her shoulder. "I love you, Baby. Don't let me down. Come with me—now."

Kate studied him.

His eyes were pleading with her. His cheeks were bright red. Holden had been on a roller coaster ride of mood swings for six months. Maybe he did need a change of scenery. Ava had put such a strain on their relationship, and those wounds had taken a long time to heal. Maybe a new job and a new location was just what the doctor ordered. After all, if it didn't work out, they could always come home, right? How could she deny the man that she loved her unconditional support? That's what he was asking for: unconditional support. She needed to step up to the plate.

Kate looked up at him and smiled. She brushed back a frock of hair from his soggy forehead. "Okay ...I'll be spontaneous for once in my life. I'll break it to my dad tonight, and we'll leave first thing in the morning."

Holden pressed his lips to hers. His kiss was carnal and possessive. When he pulled away, his brown eyes seared into her blue. "No. We have to leave right away—tonight."

"Oh Holden, I don't know—"

"Yes, yes you do know, Kate. You know that I love you, and you have to trust me." With that, he pushed her away. Turning his back on her, he walked several steps down the aisle before turning back and extending his hand out to her.

Kate paused—considering.

Splaying his fingers wide, he stretched his hand out further to her.

This was it: unconditional support, unconditional trust.

On a braced breath, Kate took his hand.

Stan called to Holden, "Hey, Reese!" he yelled. "What about the program? What about my freakin' stuff?"

* * * * *

Chip had searched through-out the shed rows for Doc Spears' vet truck only to find it parked outside of the well lit Test barn. Security was usually very tight around the barn because it was the barn where the horses that win a race or horses that were under scrutiny were delivered to be drug tested. The horses were assigned a stall where the trainer could clean them up after the race. Only one person was permitted to escort the horse into the test barn, and that person was required to stay with the animal for the duration of the collecting of samples.

The horses would be walked through the barn as a cool-down, and then they would be returned to the assigned stall where a sample of the horse's urine would be collected for the tests. Some horses spent very little time in the test barn, while others would take hours of walking and cajoling before surrendering their urine. Although the hour was getting late, Chip could see that several horses still remained in the barn. He could hear the trainers and handlers whistling at them in an attempt to get them to urinate.

Through the door he could see a handler with a lofty gray Thoroughbred. He heard Doc Spears call out, "Bring that one around. Let's see if he's ready." He saw his step-brother, Tony, take the horse from the handler to deliver it to Doc.

Disgusted by the fact that the old doctor was working the test barn, Chip knew he had to wait for another opportunity. He turned to leave when he bumped into Dan Quaide.

"Whoa, sorry, Chip," Dan said.

"Is Spears workin' the test barn all night?" Chip asked.

"Yep, it was supposed to be Doc Reese, but you heard what happened at the West's stable, I'm sure. Reese probably got his hands full. I heard the horse was pretty bad off. Who the hell would do such a dirty trick?"

"Yeah, yeah, that's a shame." Chip stretched his neck to look into the barn again. "I don't see that pretty redhead that works for Spears."

"Ava? I saw her leave with her boyfriend about twenty minutes ago," Dan said. "Do you need Spears? One of my horses is in there, so I've got clearance. I can get him for you."

"No, no, I'll talk to him later. Thanks, Dan. See ya."

* * * * *

Tony handed off the lead to the big gray gelding that belonged to Dan Quaide's stable to Doc. He placed the long-handled ladle underneath the horse to catch the urine that the Thoroughbred surrendered.

"'Bout damned time," Doc groused, "you been in here for almost two hours." He poured the urine into a container and marked it. As Tony turned to lead the animal away, Doc said, "By the way, Tony, I'm changing the tests tonight. The list of drugs that we're testing for is on the desk over there. Could you bring it to me, please?"

Tony stopped dead in his tracks. The horse almost ran him over. Clenching his teeth, he shoved the horse's lead to Dan and spun around to face Doc. "Whatta ya mean, you're changing the list? You can't do that. We—we've already collected and marked a bunch of the containers. It'll back the lab up. You can't change now…we'll have to re-do all the paperwork, re-mark all the containers, that would… um…make extra work."

147

Doc looked up over his bifocals at the frustrated employee as well as several trainers who were walking-out their horses. Duane Bishop was among them. Agitation wasn't the only expression that filled the men's faces. They were also twisted with angst.

Doc lifted an eyebrow at the surly group. He announced, "I've been the state veterinarian longer than you've been alive, young man. I'm very well aware of the rules, and I can change the list as I see fit. The lab will comply with my request."

"Well…yeah…but it's gettin' awful late, Doc—"

"You're being paid for your time." Narrowing his eyes and cocking his head, Doc asked, "Is there a problem here that I'm unaware of, Tony?" He took in Tony's tightened shoulders and defensive stance.

Duane stepped forward into Doc's space. "What's the problem, Doc? You seem a bit out of sorts tonight."

"I'm always out of sorts, Duane, and if you don't back up a step I'm gonna tag your horses to be tested every single time they run a race. That should lighten my mood considerably." Scanning the area at the men who were groaning and shaking their heads, Doc added, "In fact I'm going to request testing for everything tonight. Batten down the hatches, Tony, it's gonna be a long-ass night. You got a problem with that?"

Leading his horse toward the door, Dan called over his shoulder, "I wouldn't screw with him, Tony.

He might ask you to pee into that big ol' ladle!" Chuckling, he lead his horse from the test barn into the darkness.

Tony's eyes flicked to Dan and then back to Doc whose lips slowly curled into a cool grin. "The list, Tony, I asked you to get the list from the desk, thank you."

Letting out a disgusted breath, Tony's shoulders dropped. Running a harried hand through his dark hair, he started toward the desk.

Doc added, "Oh, we're gonna need a fresh pot of coffee, too."

Nasty comments could be heard from the group of disgruntled trainers. Tony fingered his cell phone in his hip pocket and then thought better of it.

* * * * *

Kate rushed to her father's desk and grabbed a piece of paper. She sat in her father's leather chair and began to write a note, while Holden furtively looked out the window. He could see the horse trailer parked outside the barn. The lights were on. He was thankful that Kate felt so rushed that she hadn't asked to go see her father. He knew Eric and Mike would soon leave the barn. He needed to hurry her along.

Kate's voice broke his train of thought. "I don't know why you won't just let me give Dad a call, Holden."

"Because he'd talk you right out of it, that's why."

"They're down at the barn. I could stop in and tell him, and we could check on Shady Deal before we go."

"Kate..."

"Okay, okay. Geesh, you're not giving me much credit."

"No," he said, "I'm not taking any chances." He tried to make it seem like a joke.

Giggling, Kate tossed the pen aside and placed the note in the middle of the desk. "Let me grab a few things, and I'll be ready. Oh, and grab my back-pack too, please." She pushed from the seat to make her way to the foyer.

Holden blocked her exit. He grabbed her by the arm and pulled her to him. He kissed her. Then, pressing his forehead against hers, he murmured, "You mean everything to me, Kate."

Smiling, she caressed his cheek with the back of her fingers. "Are you feeling okay? You're awfully clammy."

"I'm just anxious to get on the road." He whirled her around to give her a swat on the derrière. "So hurry it up. I'll be waiting in your car."

Kate hurried through the foyer and up the stair-case. Holden listened to her footsteps until she reached the hallway before making his way to the desk, grabbing the note, and shoving it into his pocket.

Looking around the room, his eyes fell upon her backpack that she'd thrown onto the sofa. Hurried, he rifled through it until he found her cell phone. Taking his cell from his pocket, he returned to the desk and opened the lower left drawer. While tossing them in, he noticed Eric's Glock 19 in the bottom of the drawer.

Holden couldn't help but be reminded of his conversation with Kate's father not long ago when he was asking for the man's blessing to take Kate's hand in marriage.

"Are you a man of integrity, Dr. Reese?" he remembered Eric asking him while he wiped down the barrel of the Glock.

Holden was certain that indeed he used to be a man of integrity. Remorse washed through him that he was no longer the kind of man that Eric West wanted for his daughter—not since his life had become entwined with Chip Walker's. Thinking back on the conversation, he realized that Eric never actually gave his blessing—only a warning that he had better take very good care of Kate.

With every intention of taking good care of the woman he loved, Holden had to distance himself from Chip Walker so that no one could claim that he was in on what the slimy bastard was about to do. Holden grabbed the gun and searched the drawer for ammo. Nothing. He yanked the lower drawer open on the left. Letting out a relieved breath, he found a magazine in the bottom of the drawer. Eric was a cautious man. He didn't store the ammo with the gun. Holden shoved the magazine into the Glock and deposited it in the inside pocket of his jacket.

Kate called down the stairs, "Are we stopping at your apartment for your stuff?"

Holden froze. "Ahhh...I don't need much. Whatever I need, we can pick up along the way."

He rushed to the window to check on Eric and Mike. The lights in the barn were still on. Good. Looking around the study, he let out a sigh and turned out the lights.

~ NINE ~

Stella leaped onto the black satin comforter that was in a tangle. Purring, the white Persian nuzzled the bottom of her mistress's feet. Ava's toes curled. Moaning softly, she snuggled closer into Lugowski's bare chest while the cat made herself comfortable in the curve of Ava's knee.

Candles burning on the vanity and windowsill sent a waft of mulberry spice to veil the scent of sex. The moon filtered through the shade to cast ashen shadows across the bed while a jazz CD crooned from the living room.

Staring at the ceiling, Lugowski wondered how the Wests were connected to the drug ring at the track.

Surely, that's what the horse's beating was all about. There was no way Mike was buying illegal drugs. He wasn't a Mike West fan, but the man had honor. He wasn't a cheater. So it couldn't be that he owed money to a pusher.

Did Mike see or hear or know something that he wasn't supposed to? He was hoping that Jack Haliday's undercover agent would come up with some answers from within the underbelly of the backside.

Ava's fingers caressed his chiseled chest. Vibrating against the empty wine glasses on the nightstand, Lugowski's cell phone began to ring.

Ava groaned. "Honestly, can't we go one whole night without someone killing their wife, co-worker, or the pizza delivery boy?"

Lugowski reached for the phone. He checked the screen: Jack Haliday. Without hesitation, he put the phone to his ear. "What've ya got, Jack?"

"Dave should've checked in by now. He leans toward the rookie side when it comes to experience, so I'm a bit concerned. Even if he doesn't have anything solid, he should've checked in. I've tried calling him and I get nothing. I'm going to the track to check on him or kick his ass. I haven't decided which. You want in on this?"

"I'll meet you at the security gate in thirty." Lugowski thumbed the END button. When he turned, he was greeted by Ava's scowl. He kissed her lightly on the forehead. "I'm sorry, Baby, but this is important."

"Isn't it always?"

"I suppose so." He slipped from her embrace.

Her hand fell onto his pillow with a slap. The mattress dipped and then sprung back as he pushed away. Pulling the sheets over her breasts, she watched his naked form search the pile of clothes on the vanity chair until he found his boxer briefs.

His body was slim and tight. The tribal tattoo on his right shoulder always intrigued her. The jagged curves of the dark design curled around his muscles and moved with their every flexion. She had decided long ago that it was very sexy and masculine in the most primal way.

Now that the boyfriend had evacuated the bed, Stella padded across Ava's tummy to cuddle in her arms.

Pulling on his socks, Lugowski said, "It's late anyway, you'll be sleeping soon."

Stroking the cat's fluffy back, she muttered, "Maybe, or I could do some window shopping on E-Harmony."

* * * * *

Dirty, tired, and sweaty, Ramon and Parker continued the task of digging a hole large enough for two bodies after Chip had returned from his unsuccessful errand of finding Doc Spears alone. He was hopeful to put three bodies in the hole. Not happening.

Retiring to the office to watch over their hostages, Chip was pleased with the two huge men's progress in only two hours. They had removed the stall mats, stacking them outside the stall. The hole was rather large and deep. They had struggled to dig with only a single flashlight as a guide, sometimes hitting each other with an elbow or the handle of a shovel. Tempers were escalating like the mounds of dirt collected along the back wall and the left side of the stall.

Finally, Parker decided he'd had enough. It was time to rid the world of Shane West and Dave Blake. He chucked his shovel out of the hole against the corner of the back wall and then he climbed out of the damp abyss to inform Chip that the job was finished—whether he liked it or not.

Ramon dragged along behind him toward the office. Edginess bled through his tone, when he stated, "We gotta get this done quicker, man. That dude's a cop, and they're gonna come lookin'."

Pitching him an impassive look, Parker pushed through the office door. Chip was seated at his desk with his leg propped up. His flashlight and gun were trained on Shane and Dave. Shane sat in the corner of the room. Both sleeves from his shirt were ripped off. He held the strips of clothing tautly against Dave's shoulder in an effort to keep the bleeding at bay. Fighting to hold on to consciousness, Dave lay across his lap. He was shaking in excruciating pain.

Shane tried to keep his hands as steady as possible while he held the fabric against him. Part of Dave's shoulder bone stuck out of the gunshot wound.

"We're done. Let's get this party started," Parker stated, succinct.

"Good."

"What about Spears?" Ramon asked.

"We'll have to deal with him later." Chip waved the gun at Shane, "Let's go, I haven't had dinner yet, and I'm starvin'."

Shane carefully helped Dave to a sitting-up position. Dave grunted and winced in pain when Shane helped him to stand. "Lean on me." Shane draped Dave's good arm over his shoulder.

Dave had no choice. He was completely drained of strength and fighting to keep aware of his surroundings. Parker and Ramon stepped into the aisle, while Chip stepped aside allowing them to exit the office. Each stride was slow and measured. Outnumbered, no weapons, and a seriously injured man on his arm, Shane was praying that someone would show up before they made it to the stall, except soon they were standing at the stall door.

Chip flashed his light into the hole. "Looks official. After we put them in, we'll cover them over, put the stall mats back, replace the bedding, and put a horse in here. It'll be like nothin' ever happened." Smiling, he turned to Shane. "Kinda cool, don't you think, West? I mean all these years you worked with horses, now your final resting place will be under one. What do they call that? A cruel irony." Chuckling, he waved the gun in Shane's face. "Go on. Get in there."

Shane's lips curled in disdain. Ramon shoved him, hard. "You heard him! Getta move on!"

Lugging Dave, Shane hobbled along the stall wall while peering into the dark pit. He had to be cautious. The rim was narrow and slick from the disheveled dirt. If they slipped into the hole, all hope would be diminished. He hauled Dave all the way to the back corner, where he leaned against the wall for a breath. He bumped something hard and metal against the wall that he was leaning on.

Stealthily, he let his hand drop down behind him to feel the object. Soon, he realized that it was a shovel.

Chip, Ramon, and Parker crowded carefully into the stall around the perimeter of the hole. The cloying smell of damp earth and horse manure filled the close space. With the hole taking up so much of the area, Chip was forced to stand near the back corner with Dave and Shane.

Dave coughed. His knees were buckling. Shane inclined him against the wall in hopes that he could hold a bit of his own weight.

Splaying his fingers wide against the rough wood, Dave clung to the wall. The burning pain in his shattered shoulder was so fierce that he almost welcomed a bullet to take it all away.

Keeping his eyes trained on Chip, Shane wrapped his fingers around the handle of the shovel.

* * * * *

With a cigarette dangling from his lip, Lugowski pulled into the stable gate. He could see Jack talking with the security guard through the window of the guard shack. He slid from his SUV, pitched the cigarette aside, and went inside. The guard and Jack turned when he walked through the door of the tiny building.

Jack reported, "The guard hasn't seen Dave all day."

"He's on the suspension list. He got into a fist fight with a trainer, Stan Urick," the guard explained.

"Maybe we should talk with Mr. Urick," Lugowski suggested.

"Let's go," Jack said.

"According to my sign-in sheet, Stan's still here somewhere. His stable is in row F," the guard told them.

When Jack opened the door, a young girl on a pony rode up to the shack. "Whatta ya want?" the guard asked.

"Chip Walker got any horses in tonight?" she wanted to know.

Jack and Lugowski waited while the guard flipped several pages on his clipboard before answering. "Nope, why?"

"I seen flashlights movin' around inside his barn. You'd better check it out. Someone might be stealin' his stuff, or beatin' up on one of his horses, like what happened to the West's." She had a hint of urgency in her voice.

"Did she say Walker Stables?" Lugowski asked.

"Yeah," the girl said.

Lugowski yanked his badge from his belt and shoved it into the guard's face. "Lieutenant Carl Lugowski of the Rosemount Police, I want you to lockdown the stable area until further notice. You got that?"

The guard's eyes were as big as cue balls. His jaw dropped. "Yes, sir!"

"What barn?" Lugowski asked him.

"Last barn on the left, shed row D."

Jack was already to the door of his black SUV.

Jogging past the girl on her pony, Lugowski turned and pointed a warning finger at her. "You stay right there, Miss." He jumped into the passenger seat of Jack's vehicle.

The old metal gate bumped and groaned while it swung open. Turning his headlights down to the parking lights, Jack steered the vehicle through the rows of stables while looking for D. Most of the stables were dark, but some still had activity.

They could see silhouettes of stable workers hand walking Thoroughbreds or dumping wheelbarrows into the manure bins. Finally, they came upon the long row with the large faded letter D painted on the end-wall.

Jack parked the SUV behind a manure bin. They got out of the vehicle and crept around the bin where they could see down through the row. All the stables in row D were dark. Three manure bins sat with long distances between each in the middle of the roadway that separated the row C from D. At the very end of the row, as the guard stated, they saw the ornate sign that read Walker Stables.

Drawing his gun, Jack hitched his chin toward the first manure bin. Lugowski nodded. Staying low, the two men jogged to the first bin. Seeing no threat, they made their way to the second, and finally to the third. Ducking behind the bin, they peered out at Walker Stable. Indeed, they could see the soft glow of a light beam moving about, as the pony girl had described.

"Something's going on in there," Jack said, "and if it were the business of horses, the lights would be on."

"That's what I'm thinking," Lugowski agreed.

Gauging in the stable, they saw the main door with the sign hanging on a wrought iron pole. Approximately fifty feet further down was another door. Did it lead to the same stable? All the stables were in a line. There were many doors.

Jack said, "There can't be only one entrance. That would be against code. By process of elimination, I say that door is the second entrance, right?"

"I think so," Lugowski said, "I'll go in the door to the right, you take the left."

Nodding, Jack scrambled across the roadway toward the door while sucking against the wall next to it.

Almost in choreographed synchronization, Lugowski made haste to his assigned entrance. Holding their guns to their chests, Jack meticulously cracked open the door. He could hear tense voices wafting down the barn aisle. He gave Lugowski a signal that he could hear movement, and that he was going inside.

Taking hold of the door near him, Lugowski nodded to Jack in kind.

Once inside, they could see the movement of the flashlights coming from a stall almost dead center of the stable. They could hear men's voices and almost make out their words. Lugowski and Jack crept along the walls. Jack ducked behind a wheelbarrow that was standing on end against the wall, while Lugowski took cover behind a stack of hay bales. Keeping eye contact, they strained to listen to determine what the situation was, and how many bad guys they would have to deal with.

* * * * *

Dave couldn't stand any longer. The pain was so intense and his strength could no longer sustain his weight. He sunk to his knees.

"Okay, let's do this. Get in the hole, West," Chip turned toward Parker. "We'll shoot him down there, and then —"

Swinging the shovel hard, Shane slammed it into Chip's chest!

With a grunt, Chip folded in half and plunged into the ditch. His gun dropped from his hand to fall into the dirt.

Dave's eyesight was fuzzy, but he knew what the object was. Propping his body against the wall, he began groping in the wet dirt with his good hand for the gun.

Taking advantage of the surprise, Shane whipped the shovel again to hit Ramon across the face. Ramon's head bounced off the wall. Stunned, he managed to hold onto his gun, and his consciousness. Screaming and cursing, Chip was clawing at the walls of the dark hole to get to the top. Parker tried to get past Ramon while Shane whipped the shovel back and forth like a sword. Ducking and bobbing, Parker was unable to take aim.

Dave managed to grab the gun, except his hand was shaky and it wasn't his shooting hand. With his eyesight blurry and his hand unsteady, he tried to take aim at one of the huge men, and not to hit Shane in the effort.

Shane couldn't keep the fight up much longer. He was running out of real estate. Ramon and Parker were pushing him closer and closer to the corner, while he was aware of Dave's presence near his feet. He had to take a chance.

Lunging forward to get Ramon's gun, Shane's foot drew close to the edge of the hole. Chip grabbed hold, and pulled him into the pit. Shane landed on his back with a hard thud. Jumping down from the greasy wall, Chip kicked him in the ribs—hard.

Suddenly, another body fell into the pit. Parker had grabbed the gun from Dave's hand and then kicked him into the hole. Dave screamed in agony when he hit the ground.

Parker dropped to his stomach. He reached his hand down to Chip to help him out of the pit.

Filthy, sweaty, and livid, Chip snatched the gun from Parker's hand. His face was twisted into a poisonous scowl as he pointed it into the pit. Breathlessly, he stated, "You've got balls, I'll give you that much!"

Knowing they were beat, and knowing that no one was coming to help them, Shane accepted his fate. This was the moment; this was how his life was going to come to an end. Lying on the floor of the pit, he closed his eyes waiting for the fatal shot.

"Police! Drop your weapons!" Lugowski shouted as he stepped into the doorway.

Parker grabbed the gun from Chip's hand. He whipped it around toward Lugowski only to be greeted by a bullet to the chest. Parker flailed backward against the wall, sliding down into the corner, his chin tucked to his chest—dead.

Chip threw his hands in the air in surrender.

Shifting fitfully from one foot to the other, Ramon danced in panic.

Jack appeared at Lugowski's side with his gun trained on Ramon along with the lieutenant's.

Lugowski repeated. "Put your gun down!"

Sweat trickled down Ramon's bruised face. His eyes were swollen almost shut from the impact of the shovel when Shane had hit him. "No way! I ain't goin' back to no prison cell!"

"Put your gun down!" Lugowski insisted. "Now!"

Chip stared at Ramon in complete bafflement. "C'mon, dude, it's over. Put it away."

Ramon shook his head. Seemingly disoriented from panic, he pointed the gun at Lugowski and then at Chip. He was in a standoff that he knew he couldn't win. He stuck the gun in his mouth and pulled the trigger!

Wincing, Chip ducked away as the top of Ramon's head exploded into bloody brain matter. His body plunged into the hole.

Ramon's maimed carcass fell next to Shane with a hard thud. Shane was on his knees trying to care for Dave. Sickened by the sight, he turned away and called up the dirt wall. "We need medics right away! Dave's been shot!"

~ TEN ~

Eric paced back and forth in the dimly lit viewing room that looked into the interrogation room at the Rosemount Police Department. Running his hand over his stiff neck, he looked up at the clock on the wall: two o'clock in the morning. Frustration burned through him. He leaned against the wall to watch Jack Haliday question Chip Walker. They seemed to be going in circles and getting nowhere.

Lugowski slipped through the door with a coffee in each hand. His shirt was unbuttoned down to the second button, and his tie hung loose below the third. His eyes were bruised with fatigue. "I spoke with the hospital. Dave Blake is still in surgery. They will have to rebuild his shoulder. He'll be down for a while." He handed Eric one of the coffees.

"Is Shane still at the hospital?" Eric asked.

"Yeah, the nurse said he's sitting in the surgical waiting area, but he's fine." Lugowski lifted the coffee to his lips. He measured Eric's distraught expression. He had witnessed that expression on many a father's face, and many times the outcome was just as disastrous as the expression.

The uniforms that showed up at the scene at the racetrack had found out from the security guard that Holden and Kate had left the track in her Mustang around nine o'clock. They were aware that Holden was involved in the drug ring, and that he had run. Lugowski was positive that Kate was ignorant of the entire drug activity, and he was fairly certain that Holden would not harm her. At least he was praying that he wouldn't.

"Don't worry, Mr. West," Lugowski said. "We've put an APB on Kate's Mustang. After the arrests, I had an opportunity to speak to the pony girl who told me about the strange activity at Walker Stables. She told me that she saw Holden's truck at Stan Urick's stable earlier in the evening. He's most likely the last person to have seen them before they left the racetrack. I've sent an officer to his home to pick him up so we can question him. He may have had a conversation or overheard a conversation about where Holden and Kate were going. In any case, we're covering all the bases."

"Thank you, Lieutenant."

"I'd better get in there and help Jack with this interrogation before Walker's lawyer shows up. Lord knows they always do."

Lugowski pressed through the door. Jack was leaning against the cold block wall. His jacket was slung over the back of the metal chair at the table, and his sleeves were rolled to his elbows. Lugowski measured Chip's posture and demeanor. He was slumped in the chair with his arms folded over his chest. His long legs were stretched out with his left ankle crossed over his right. Chip's expression was impassive. He was cool and collected.

Jack looked over his shoulder at Lugowski when he came through the door. "Gee whiz, Lugowski, how many years do ya get for shooting a police officer?"

Lugowski took the chair across the table from Chip. "Oooh, fifteen...maybe twenty, depending on the judge's mood."

Chip's eyes rotated toward Lugowski. He huffed. "I didn't shoot the cop. That was Parker."

Lugowski took a sip of his coffee. Shrugging, he pointed out, "Parker's not here. Neither is Ramon. Hey Jack, do you think Dave's gonna remember exactly who shot him?"

Jack lifted a shoulder.

Lugowski smiled at Chip. "Yeah, I don't think so either. Plus we've got Shane West as a witness to the entire incident, and that's not the story that he's telling. Is it Jack?"

"Hey, I found them in my office stealin' stuff. Besides, I wasn't gonna really shoot them, I was just messin' with them, you know, teach them a lesson. But then Parker got a little worked up."

"Is that so?" Jack said, "I believe him, Lugowski, just like I believe everything that goes on in those reality TV shows. I suppose the big hole in the horse stall was just for special affects."

Lugowski snorted. "Let's talk about Dr. Holden Reese."

Chip's eyes were seething at the lieutenant. His voice flattened. "What about him?"

"Where is he?" Lugowski said. "We'd like to talk to him."

"How the hell should I know?"

Jack walked up behind him. Bending down, he spoke directly into his ear. "Cuz your cell phone records indicate that you had a conversation with Dr. Reese right before this all went down. We know that Reese was writing the scripts, Walker."

"You mean the scripts that Dave stole, without a search warrant? Those scripts?"

"Uh, oh, he's got us right where he wants us, Jack." Lugowski leaned over the table. "While that might cause us some problems, it doesn't change the fact that you shot a cop and tried to kill Shane West. And when we start interrogating horse trainers, there's gonna be a whole lotta finger pointing going on, and guess who they're going to be pointing at? Now, just in case you didn't hear the question: where is Dr. Reese?"

Lugowski searched his face for clues. Chip didn't give any away.

Instead he said, "He didn't say where he was goin'. He's probably with that blonde chick."

Jack straightened. "You mean Kate West?"

"Yeah, that's her. Reese said he was leavin'. That's it. He didn't tell me where."

"What was Dr. Reese's payoff for providing the scripts?" Lugowski asked.

The question was moot. The door whooshed open. A tall thin balding man wearing a dark suit and carrying a briefcase breezed into the room.

Lugowski muttered, "Right on cue."

"Thank you for keeping my client comfortable, gentlemen," he said. "I'm Randal Gold, Mr. Walker's attorney. I'd like to have a moment or two of his time."

Taking the last gulp of his coffee, Lugowski remained in the chair. Jack took to leaning against the wall. Gold shot them both a speaking glance and then backed it up with, "Alone."

* * * * *

The sweat continued to dribble down Holden's temples. The night had turned chilly so the windows in the Mustang were up except for the small crack in his window. Following Kate's hand-held GPS system, he drove. Avoiding the main highways, he used as many two lane and back roads that the device would provide.

He glanced across the cab.

Sleeping, Kate's head was tilted to the side. A frock of her hair lay across her cheek. She was snuggled in a cozy fleece throw that Jen had given her for Christmas. The shadows of the night swept over the delicate plains of her lovely face. Her hoop earrings glinted when the headlights from a passing car sliced through the windshield.

Holden reached for his cell phone several times only to be reminded that he'd tossed them in the drawer of Eric's desk. Repeatedly, his left hand would wander from the steering wheel to finger the Glock 19 that he'd retrieved from that same desk.

He looked down at the GPS. They had been on the road for close to three hours.

They were almost to Columbus, Ohio.

* * * * *

There was little reason to hang around the police station. Chip had lawyered up. The interrogation came to a halt, and even though they had a pile of evidence to hold Chip for a very high bond, Eric felt that they had gotten exactly nowhere. Where were Kate and Holden? Chip had to know.

Eric was exhausted when he came through the front door. The grandfather clock in the foyer greeted him with the three a.m. chimes. The soft glow from the brass lamp on his desk in the study filtered into the foyer. He made his way to the desk to turn the lamp off only to find Jen asleep on the sofa.

The sight of her urged a smile on his lips. Slowly, he eased down on the sofa next to her and caressed her cheek with the pad of his thumb.

Flinching, she sat up onto her elbow. "Eric...did they find Kate and Holden? Did you bring Shane home with you?"

"What time is it?" Mike asked in a raspy voice from the winged-back chair across the room. He ran his fingers through the thick nest of curls on his head as he sat up.

"It's three a.m.," Eric said. "No, they have not found Kate and Holden, and Shane is still at the hospital with Dave Blake. I spoke with him on the phone a little while ago. He wants to stay with Dave until family shows up or whatever happens. I told him he should come home and get some rest, but you know Shane, once he's made his mind up there's no reasoning with him."

"I think it's honorable of him to stay with his friend," Jen said. "If he's not home by morning, I'll run some clean clothes to him, and some apple muffins that I made while I've been waiting for you to come home." She attempted to get up from the sofa. "Would you like some..."

Eric gently tugged her back in place. "I'm not very hungry, Jen. I'm going to take a shower, and then I'm going to try to get some sleep. Although I don't know how successful I'll be. I don't think that Holden would do anything to harm Kate, but how can we be sure?"

"You need some sleep. I should go home—"

"You're not driving home at this hour, Ms. Fleming. You're staying the night."

"I'll stay in Kate's room." She tugged him to his feet. "C'mon, let's get you upstairs."

"That's my cue," Mike said, lifting from the chair. "I'm heading home."

Hand in hand Eric and Jen walked Mike to the foyer.

Mike nodded at his father and gave Jen a peck on the cheek. "See you in the morning." He slipped out the door.

Eric dropped the dead bolt into place and turned to Jen. "I'll be up in a moment. With everything that has happened in last few days, I just feel the need to have my gun closer to me than in my desk."

Jen's face flooded with concern. "I don't blame you, I suppose. After what happened to your horse and now this whole ordeal with Chip Walker, but please be careful with that thing, it scares me to death."

Though his eyes burned with fatigue and his body felt like it had been hit by a truck, Eric managed a half-smile. "Why would it scare you? I thought you were going to sleep in Kate's room."

"Yeah, right. I'm pretty sure Mike wasn't buying that line either," she said over her shoulder while climbing up the staircase.

Eric chuckled to himself as he made his way around the desk and opened the lower left drawer. His eyes narrowed and his amusement with Jen's comments was instantly dashed.

The Glock was not in the drawer, yet two cell phones were. He bent down and snatched them from the bottom of the drawer. Immediately, he recognized Kate's glitzy zebra striped phone cover. What was Kate's phone doing in his desk? He studied the other phone. He turned it on and scrolled through the contacts. It was Holden's.

Tossing the phones onto the desk, he yanked the lower drawer on the right open only to discover that his ammunition was gone as well. Trepidation skittered up his spine. This put a whole new twist on the situation.

Quickly, he searched the desk and the floor around it for a note or anything Kate may have left behind. Nothing. Kate would never leave without letting him know. She always had her cell with her.

What troubled him the most was the presence of Holden's phone and the absence of his gun.

God almighty.

Suddenly Eric felt breathless. Did Kate run with him? It couldn't be. Kate would never run off leaving her brother in such a dire situation. He refused believe it. Even if Kate didn't know about Shane, she would have never condoned drugging horses. He sunk into his chair behind the desk. Kate was a stubborn woman. Did Holden force her to go with him? If she put up any kind of a fight, would Holden hurt her? After finding his handgun and ammo missing and the cell phones in his desk drawer, he wasn't so sure.

He had already allowed the scenario of Kate being forced to go with Holden into consideration a thousand times over while he paced the floors at the police station, and now it looked as though it was more than a simple scenario—it could possibly be a hostage situation.

Lifting his face toward the ceiling he squeezed his eyes closed, Dear God, please keep her safe. Keep my Kate safe.

"Eric...are you all right? I thought you were coming right up." Jen said from the study doorway. "What's wrong? You're face is beet red."

Yanking his cell phone from his hip pocket, Eric said, "I'm calling Lugowski."

~ ELEVEN ~

After filling up at a run-down gas station in a dusty little town just over the state line of Kentucky, Holden paid the attendant with cash. Waiting for Kate to emerge from the restroom, he slid into the driver's seat of the Mustang. He was feeling drained of strength from anxiety and the all night drive.

Holden leaned out of the window and said to the attendant, "I'm assuming there aren't any hotels around here, right?"

"Ya shouldn't assume nothin', cuz that just makes an ass outta you and me." The man laughed and slapped his knee at the bad joke, as if it were an original. Noticing Holden's lack of humor, he said, "Sure there is! Drive down this road about a mile at at the first stop sign take a left. About a mile and a half, you'll find Gertie's Bed and Breakfast. It's a pretty nice place. Boy oh boy, the food sure is good.

I have breakfast there at least twice a week. Ya can't miss if you go there."

Kate dropped into her seat and closed the door.

Holden waved at the man. "Okay, thanks." He started the car and pulled out of the station onto a two-lane road.

"Where are we?" Kate asked.

"We crossed the Kentucky state line about thirty miles back."

Kate took in the rural surroundings. "Surely, this can't be the most efficient route to Houston. Is that GPS working right? This can't be a very direct route."

"I got a little off course. Do you mind if I ask why you don't have an on-board GPS system?"

"That would've added like fifteen hundred bucks to the price of the car. I don't mean to be cheap, but I already owned this one." She studied him for a few moments. "Are you okay? You've been sweating ever since we left."

"Eh, I'm really tired from all the driving, and I'm a little worried about the interview. I'll be okay."

"It's a long way to Texas, Holden. If you don't relax you'll be nothing but a puddle by the time we get there."

"No worries." He rolled the car to a stop at a stop sign. "There's a bed and breakfast up this road. We can grab some sleep for a couple of hours and then get back at it."

"Great, I can't wait to get into a shower."

"Mmmm, that makes two of us."

"I thought you said you were tired."

"I'm never too tired." He shot his finger into the air. "I know... you can be a tourist from France that wandered into the wrong room, and I find you in my shower. The communication is a little dicey, but we both want a shower...badly."

"A French tourist in this backwoods town in Kentucky?" Laughing, Kate threw her head back. "Oh, Holden, you and your fantasies. You may not be tired, but you sure can be tiring!"

With a salacious smile stretched across his face, Holden pumped his eyebrows up and down while using a very bad French accent. *"Oui, oui, mademoiselle."*

* * * * *

Gertie's Bed and Breakfast was a huge two-story cedar cabin nestled against a backdrop of Sassafras trees. The cabin flaunted a welcoming porch that took in the entire front of the building. Huge baskets filled with lazy green ferns hung between each post, and large comfy rocking chairs were lined up all the way across the porch. The air was crisp and fresh with a subtle hint of Sassafras.

Holden was relieved. He was worried that the bed and breakfast would be a little less than upscale. He was pleasantly surprised.

Kate smiled at the bucolic setting. Holden wrapped his arm around Kate's shoulder as they climbed the steps onto the porch and through the front door.

They were greeted by an enormous stone fireplace that climbed all the way to the peak of the large registration area. The hard wood floors gleamed. As if inviting guests to sit and relax, a comfortable couch and two stuff chairs were placed in front of the fireplace.

Off to the left was a spacious dining area. Small decorative lanterns adorned each table, which had four puritan-style chairs. Burnt orange tablecloths accentuated the rich tones of the cedar planking that made up the walls. Several wagon-wheel chandeliers hung in the room to give it a down-home atmosphere. High above the tables, deer and elk heads were mounted on the walls.

The registration desk was off to the right beside a wide sweeping staircase flanked with chunky oak railings. The older gray-haired woman who manned the desk did not appreciate the assumption that Holden made by calling her Gertie. Her brows fell into a disparaging "V" as she informed him, "My name is Clara. Gertie Hanson has been dead for over fifty years, God rest her soul, now what can I do for you, young man?"

Furtively, Holden looked over his shoulder. Kate was checking out the fireplace and the sight-seeing brochures in the wrought iron rack positioned on the hearth, while stroking a fat calico cat that had appeared from its sleeping spot behind the display. He turned back to Clara. "I'd like a room, please."

Clara tapped at her computer. "Name?"

Again, Holden checked out Kate's location in the room. The cat was then in her arms. She tickled its ears. He said, "Holden...Re—Redman."

Over her bifocals, Clara eyed him for a moment. With a lift of her shoulder, she said, "Okay. What credit card will you be paying with today, Mr. Redman?"

"I'll be paying cash. We won't be staying the night. We just need to crash for awhile."

"Whatever. That'll be eighty-five dollars, please."

Frowning, Holden dug into his pocket and produced the correct currency. Clara slid a key card across the counter. "Up the stairs, third room on the right."

"Thank you." Holden turned to find Kate admiring the quaint table settings. The cat was then perched on the sofa in front of the fireplace. He turned back to Clara. "Is your kitchen still open? We sure could use some breakfast."

"Oh sure, have a seat. I'll have the server bring you a menu." Clara hurried around the counter toward the dining room and through the kitchen door.

Coming up behind her, Holden wrapped his arms around Kate. He whispered into her ear, "Let's have some breakfast first and then it's the shower for you, FeFe."

Giggling, Kate tossed her backpack onto a chair and then took a seat at the table. She watched Holden drop into a chair.

He looked whiplashed from exhaustion. His eyes were bloodshot and droopy, but at least he'd stopped sweating and seemed a bit more relaxed.

Her blue eyes looked into his fatigued, worrisome brown eyes. He reached across the table to swallow her hands into his. He bit his lip and then took in a deep breath. He spoke quietly in a raspy voice, "I'm really sorry..." His words trailed off.

Her eyes narrowed from lack of understanding.

He swallowed hard. "I'm really sorry that I drug you away like I did."

"It's no biggie. I'm no worse for the wear."

"You mean everything to me, Kate. I want you with me always, no matter what happens." He sucked in a quivering breath that was almost sob-like.

Kate blinked back. "That sounds a bit melodramatic." She squeezed his hands. "You know that I'm always here for you, Holden. We got past the Ava thing. It was tough, but we made it. I'm sure we can handle just about anything that is thrown at us now."

"I hope so," he murmured. He wasn't sure. He wasn't sure at all.

Once again she could see his angst bubbling to the surface. "Are you sure you're okay?"

He scrubbed a hand across his bristly chin, through his hair, and down the nape of his neck. "It's the sleep depravation talking. Don't mind me."

* * * * *

With their bellies full of a generous homemade breakfast, Kate and Holden climbed the staircase. Holden unlocked the door with the key and held it open for Kate. The room was as beautifully rustic as the downstairs.

The king-size bed was made of giant logs that had been planed and then carved with images of deer, raccoons, pheasants, and rabbits. A thick wool Indian blanket trimmed with fringe lay across the bed to welcome them. The huge suede jute bags that served as plump pillows looked delightfully cozy.

The headboard sported a wide shelf that had lines with fat cream-colored pillar candles that were secured into drilled holders. Floor to ceiling windows looked out over a serene lake where Canadian geese were gliding along the water.

"Oh, it's just beautiful," Kate gasped.

"It's very nice. Now go get the water good and hot in the shower. I'll join you in a few minutes."

Holden backed it up with a quick swat on her tight derrière.

Kate tossed her backpack onto the bed. She took another moment to drink in the glorious view beyond the windows before going into the bathroom and closing the door behind her.

Holden listened for the water to pulse against the shower walls, and for the sound of Kate moving about the room. Her boots clunked to the floor. Quickly, he snatched up the telephone on the nightstand, unhooked it from the wall, and tossed it under the bed. He drew the blinds closed to darken the room and to shut out the world.

Feeling the weight of the gun in his jacket, he looked around the room for a place to stash it. The last thing he wanted was for Kate to realize that he had a gun, or worse recognize the gun as her father's. Since they were only staying at the B&B for a couple of hours, they wouldn't be using any of the drawers, so he opened a drawer in the armoire that held the television and placed the Glock way in the back of it. He needed to make sure that he remembered to get the gun before they left. Somehow, he doubted that he'd forget.

The thick curtains made the room very dim.

Holden found a box of matches on the nightstand, so he lit most of the candles mounted on the headboard. The flickering flames tossed romantic dancing shadows across the shiny oak planking throughout the room. They served as a good distraction to boot.

He sank onto the edge of the bed and tried to rub away the stress in his neck.

The sound of the shower curtain pushing across the rod alerted him that Kate was stepping into the shower.

Holden eddied out of his T-shirt and dropped it to the floor. He yanked his boots from his feet and pitched them into a corner along with his socks. Standing, he unbuckled his belt, unzipped his jeans and let them pool at his feet. Stepping out of his jeans, he crossed the room. Wearing only his boxer briefs, he slipped through the bathroom door.

An ashen haze of steam greeted him. "Are you ready for company, my little French wench?" he teased.

Kate peeked from behind the curtain. "I thought I was a French tourist. Suddenly, I've been downgraded to a common wench? What's that all about?"

The right side of Holden's mouth kicked up. He slipped his boxers off to allow his erection to spring free.

"Never mind, I'm ready." Smiling, Kate ducked behind the curtain.

Holden stepped into the hot spray. He took a moment to let the water douse him. In tiny rippling rivers, it dribbled over every defined and vibrant muscle of his body. He closed his eyes in an attempt to let it wash away the angst and the horrid thoughts of the mess that he'd left behind at Keystone Downs. His wet hair flattened against his head.

Suddenly, he felt Kate's hands slathering his chest with a honeysuckle scented body wash. It felt so good to let her wash him. It was almost healing. He let her tender touch envelope him in the love that he knew belonged to him alone.

He breathed it in.

Kate West was the only thing that he had done right in his life in a long time. The only good decision he'd made. She was the light at the end of his very dark lonely tunnel.

The intoxicating sent of honeysuckle and Kate's sultry caress plunged him into a storm of need to touch her, and to be as close to her as he possibly could get. He pulled her to him and covered her mouth with his—pressing his tongue into her mouth to taste her. Fisting his fingers through the long wet strands of her hair, he held her in place to let the water rush over them. He pushed his arousal against her tummy.

Kate wrapped her arms around his neck—pressing up on her toes to get as much from his possessive kiss that she could devour. Holden's love making was always so primal, sexy, and sometimes a little rough. Cowboy rough. Right now, it almost seemed like a desperate passion unleashing itself under the cleansing stream of the water. She wasn't sure what was going on inside him.

Holden could be fun loving and carefree one moment, and a sack of distraction and angst the next. This time, he wasn't fun loving or distracted, rather there seemed to be a consuming need bursting from him. His touch wasn't gentle—it was ravenous.

Tightening his grip on her hair, Holden pulled her head back to give him access to her neck. He kissed and nipped his way to her shoulders.

Gradually, he loosened his grip as he dragged his hands down her spine until they cupped her rear. Lifting her, he urged her to wrap her legs around him so he could enter that warm place where he could capture the pleasure and release and replete that he so desperately wanted and needed.

* * * * *

Candlelight filled the room with a soothing glow. The bathroom door opened with a whoosh. The leftover steam billowed out when Kate emerged. Using her fingers as a comb, she groomed her hair, which was still dripping droplets of moisture from its tips.

Holden watched her from under the warmth of the wool blanket. Her breasts pushed up from the white lace bra that she was wearing. She looked so sexy in the pink satin pajamas pants that hung low on her lean, shapely hips. Even the pink polish on her toenails was enough to send him into a full-blown erection.

Nestled amongst the plump pillows, he was feeling refreshed and somewhat relaxed when he noticed her scanning the room as if she were searching for something. An "ah-ha" expression crossed her face when she spotted her backpack on the floor next to the bed.

Kate unzipped the bag and rifled through it. She paused and then dug some more with a what the heck look on her face. Dropping the pack to the floor, she narrowed her eyes. She padded across the room to grab her jeans from the bathroom floor and dug through the pockets. Coming up with nothing, she appeared baffled.

"What are you looking for?" Holden finally asked.

"My cell phone. I know it was in my backpack, but I can't find it."

"Maybe you left it in the cup holder in the car."

"I don't remember putting it there. Can I use yours?"

"Sorry, FeFe, I was looking for mine earlier. I'm pretty sure that in our big hurry, I left it in the truck."

"Maybe I left mine there, too," she muttered. "Well, I'll just have to call my dad on the room phone." She came to a halt when she saw that there was no phone on the nightstand. Searching the room once more, she turned in a small circle to take in the entire space. "Where is the room phone? Don't tell me they don't have one."

Lifting to his elbows, Holden said, "Maybe not. You know how it is. Everyone has a cell phone nowadays. They probably got rid of the room phones."

"I suppose."

"We're both exhausted." He reached out and grabbed her hand. "Come to bed, Kate."

"I need to call my dad, Holden. They're going to be worried when I don't show up at the track today."

"Oh, I don't think so. They'll know you're with me, because I'm not showing up either."

"Holden, that's another thing," she said, "Our clients are going to be scrambling for veterinary services. I should make calls."

"Let those slow-paying sonofabitches scramble."

"Holden..."

"You worry too much, Kate. C'mon, we're exhausted. We'll deal with it later." Gently, he tugged her down into the bed. He rolled over to pin her to the blanket. "If I had the strength, I'd take you again." He pressed his lips to hers. When he pulled from the kiss, he caressed her cheek with his thumb while drinking in her beautiful blue eyes.

"Thank God you don't have the strength, because I certainly don't," Kate said.

"Good. No more fussing. Go to sleep so we can get back on the road in a couple of hours." She relaxed in his arms and he felt almost boneless against the mattress, until a worrisome thought crept into his mind: the GPS. If anyone decided to come looking for them, could they track them through Kate's hand-held GPS? He wasn't sure. From here on, he couldn't take the chance. Kate's breathing slowed and became shallower. She had fallen asleep.

Taking in a calming breath, Holden remembered that they had turned the GPS off when they got out of the car to come into the B&B. He was fairly certain that it couldn't be tracked if it was off. They were good to go. He closed his weary eyes and let the soothing scent of the candles and the peaceful atmosphere lull him into the rest that he so desperately needed.

~ PART THREE ~

A DARK THIN LINE

~ TWELVE ~

It had been a long night.

They had questioned Chip Walker over and over, but he was tight lipped and his attorney was like a junk-yard dog. Translation: They got squat on the horse drugging operation and, more importantly, on Holden Reese's location. Because the security guard at the track said that Holden and Kate had gone through the security gate around nine, he at least knew that Chip hadn't done away with them, they were somewhere out there. Chip had no reason not to tell them where they had gone, he was already going to be charged with attempted murder of a police officer and Shane West, so he'd come to the conclusion that Chip really didn't know where Holden and Kate were.

The police officer that Lugowski sent out to bring Stan Urick in for questioning came up empty-handed. Unable to find the man anywhere, he had left a message with his wife that they wanted to talk with him. Big deal.

Lugowski tossed in his bed all night.

Holden Reese had to know that Chip and his thugs were holding Dave Blake and Shane West at gun point with the intention of killing them and then burying them under the horse stall. Reese knew that they'd reached the end of the line with their little drug operation, and he ran. Only he took Kate West with him, and that had Lugowski at wits end. Moreover, the APB that they'd put over the wires hadn't turned up a damned thing. Kate's vehicle wasn't hooked up to an On-Star system and she hadn't opted for an on-board GPS either. What the hell? Didn't she know that it was for her own safety that she had one or the other? The West family was too damned independent for their own good.

He really didn't think that Holden would harm Kate—unless the situation got tight and he needed her as some sort of shield, bargaining chip, or, worse, he wanted to take her with him if he died.

Lugowski had seen all kinds of scenarios played out in his years as a homicide detective. This one was hitting a bit too close to home. Maybe he was too involved. Maybe he should step away. Hey, this wasn't his case to begin with. Why did he allow himself to become entangled in it?

Covering his eyes with the palms of his hands, he rolled over. He knew exactly why. It was Kate West. God, how that woman got to him. Every time she so much as stepped into a room she started his libido running at a high gear.

What the hell is the matter with him? He had the woman of his dreams: Ava. He had her exactly where he'd always wanted her from the first time he saw her: in his life and in his bed.

Why did Kate West have such a strong-hold on him?

He adjusted the pillow beneath his head and let out a self-loathing breath. It was all too complicated. She could never be his. Kate was Mike West's younger sister. She was Ava's ex-sister-in-law. Yeah, that's way out in left field.

The alarm clock screamed to jerk him from his thoughts. He swatted the off button. There was no reason to hit the snooze button. He hadn't snoozed all night.

Tossing the blankets aside, he sat up at the edge of his bed. He plucked the pack of cigarettes and his old butane lighter from the nightstand and shoved a cancer stick in his mouth. Lifting the flame to the cigarette, he inhaled deeply as if the nicotine would ease the stress he felt in his neck, shoulders, and gut.

It had all become a dark thin line.

The fact was he couldn't step back from this case. He had to see it through. He had to make sure Kate came out of this alive.

If it was the last thing that he did.

* * * * *

Jen made her way down the stark white hallway with gleaming linoleum floors toward the ICU waiting area, where a nurse had told her she would find Shane. She was amused that all the young nurses seemed to be much attuned to Shane's location. She imagined that he was being well cared for. After all, Shane was an incredibly handsome young man. She had no doubt that he was on all of the young nurse's yummy candy radar.

Nonetheless, with a bag of clean clothes and a box of apple muffins in hand she made a right into the waiting room. There he was—sprawled out on a couch, sleeping. Dressed in a pair of green scrubs, he looked quite cozy. He had several bruises on his face, but overall he looked well.

Gently, she shook his shoulder. "Shane…"

Shane's eyes jerked open as he sat up. Rubbing his eyes with one hand, while running his fingers through his tousled sandy hair with the other, he asked, "Hey Jen, what are you doing here? Is everyone okay?"

Eric had asked her not to tell Shane about Kate's situation. He didn't want to worry him, and there was nothing he could do about it anyway.

Jen smiled. "Yes, everyone is just fine. I brought you some clean clothes and some homemade apple muffins." She then noticed a small table against the wall. It was packed with food: pies, cakes, cup cakes, a half-eaten sandwich ring, and several cans of pop. Oh yeah, the nurses were taking very good care of Mr. Hot and Handsome. She couldn't help but giggle. "Hmmm, doesn't look like you need the apple muffins after all."

Shane grabbed for the box. "Are you kidding? I love your homemade stuff." He opened the box and took out a fat muffin stuffed with bits of apple.

"But it looks like you've got plenty of homemade stuff, Mr. West," she said with a grin.

"Yeah," Shane replied, "Dave would die if he knew how many pretty nurses work in this hospital. All of the nurses in the ICU are old and fat." He chuckled around a mouthful of muffin.

"How is he doing?"

"He's gonna be in a world of hurt for a long time," he said. "They had to completely rebuild his shoulder. He's got like a gazillion pins in there. They're keeping him heavily sedated. He looks pretty bad, too. But he's alive, and that's what counts."

"Are you coming home tonight?" she asked

"For a little while. Dave's parents are coming in later this afternoon. I'm going to pick them up at the airport, and I offered to let them stay with us. They can stay in Mike's old room. I know that we barely know Dave, but I feel like it's the right thing to do. I hope Dad doesn't mind."

"I'm sure he won't."

"Hey, how's Shady Deal?"

"Sounds like he and Dave are in the same boat. Like you said, he's alive and that's what counts." She took another look at the buffet table that the nurses had set up for him. "Well, I guess I didn't really need to stop in. Looks like you're being well handled." She stood and crossed the room toward the door.

"Hey, Jen," Shane called to her while grabbing for a second muffin, "did they arrest Holden?"

She hesitated. "Um...no, not yet."

"Kate's probably really upset. How's she holding up?"

Jen's mouth opened, but she couldn't find words that weren't straight-up lies. She managed a weak smile. Finally, she decided upon an ambiguous response, "She'll be okay...after a while. I've got to get to work, see you later." Hoping that was the end of the Holden and Kate questions, she turned to leave.

"Jen..." Shane called after her.

She turned.

"I'm glad you stopped by. I've been wanting to tell you that we all think you're really good for Dad. Thanks for everything."

Her cheeks felt flushed. She smiled at the sincerity in the young man's accolade. "He's a special man...with three great kids."

Just then a pretty red-headed nurse peeked into the room. She was holding a cafeteria tray with two cups of coffee and two doughnuts. "I brought you some breakfast, Shane."

Jen winked at Shane as she slipped past the nurse and into the hallway to make her way to the elevator. She chuckled when she past a blonde nurse carrying a tray with two cups of coffee and two blueberry muffins toward the room.

* * * * *

Lugowski had just poured himself a coffee in the break room when he saw an officer escort a burly man to his desk and seated him in the chair next to it. Scanning the room, the man nervously tapped his fingers on his thighs.

Stan Urick.

After stirring creamer into his coffee and wishing that he could have a cigarette to go with his breakfast, he meandered across the squad room toward the man. "Good morning," he said. "Are you Stanley Urick?"

Stan shifted in the chair. "Yeah, that's me. What's this all about?"

"Do you know a veterinarian by the name of Dr. Reese?" Lugowski eased into his chair.

"Sure. Everybody does. What about him?"

"When was the last time you saw Dr. Reese?"

"Last night, he took care of one of my horses after the races. Him and his vet assistant, Kate." Stan scratched the side of his neck. "Is...is he in some kind of trouble?"

"Maybe." Lugowski took a gulp of his coffee. He leaned back in his chair to size up the gruff-looking man. "What time was that?"

"Oh, I dunno, nine or nine thirty, maybe."

"Did Dr. Reese say that he was going on vacation or leaving Keystone Downs for any reason?"

"Ooh, I get it," Stan said. "This is about the drugs. I heard Chip Walker got arrested. The police have been combing through his stable all morning. They got that yellow tape strung all around it. Good. Put them cheatin' sonofabitches outta business, that's what I say." He declared with his chest all puffed out.

"I'm glad you feel that way, Mr. Urick. Now, did Dr. Reese mention that he was leaving Keystone Downs?"

Stan stared at his knees. He swiped his fingers across his mouth. Suddenly, his eyes brightened. He lifted his gaze to meet Lugowski's. "Yeah...seems to me like I did hear a conversation like that. He got a phone call, and then I heard him tell his assistant, Kate West, that he wanted to go to Lone Star."

"Lone Star?"

"Yeah, it's a racetrack in Texas," Stan said. "Houston, Texas. I don't think he was happy at Keystone anymore. Anyways, they left right after that. Kate didn't write me up a bill or nothin'. They just got in his truck and left." Stan crossed his arms over his chest. "Guess I won't have to pay for that vet call."

"Maybe not." Lugowski agreed. He stood up and offered his hand to Stan. "Thank you for coming in, Mr. Urick."

"That's it? That's all you needed?"

"Yes, Mr. Urick. Again, thank you."

Shrugging, Stan pushed from his seat to mosey out of the squad room.

Lugowski hurried up the stairs to the gang unit. Jack was just sitting down with his own morning java, when Lugowski approached him. "Stan Urick just left the station. He said that he heard Reese tell Kate that he wanted to go to Lone Star Racetrack in Houston."

"Sounds like he wanted to get as far away from the heat as possible," Jack said. "Well, it's the first break we've gotten. Let's map out a route to Houston and see if we can track him along the way." He took hold of his mouse and clicked it on Google maps.

"Ya know this would've been a helluva lot easier if the girl had put a GPS system in that damned Mustang."

"Tell me about it." Lugowski grumbled, as he hovered over Jack's shoulder, while he asked the search engine for directions from Rosemount, Pennsylvania, to Houston, Texas. The site brought up a map with a long blue line showing the most direct course with approximate driving times.

"That's about a twenty-one hour drive from here." Jack glanced at his watch. "They've got a good ten or twelve hour jump on us. That means they're through Columbus, Ohio, and probably well into Kentucky by now—if he's driving non-stop, which I'd bet my mama's wig that he is."

"He knew better than to go to the airport, but he may not be as panicked as we think," Lugowski said. "Eric West called me last night. He found Reese and Kate's cell phones in his desk drawer, which means he's out of communication with his buddies. He may not know that Shane and Dave are still alive and Walker's in custody. That is, if he doesn't have an-other cell with him—a burn phone maybe. Clearly, he doesn't want us to track him through the GPS in the phones. He also took Mr. West's gun—"

"He's armed?" Jack replied. "Damn."

"Well, we know the direction he's headed any-way," Lugowski said. "Let's make some plans to follow along." He pulled out his cell phone. "In the meantime, I'm going to call Mr. West to give him an update."

* * * * *

Eric, Mike, and Punch stood inside Shady Deal's stall. Punch stroked the horse's neck and shoulder. Shady Deal became rather distraught if he tried to touch his head. Since the horse arrived back at Westwood he'd spent most of his time plastered against the back wall of his stall. Any time a human came into the stall the horse would shake and cower. Punch couldn't blame him. The last human that touched his head almost killed him in a cruel and unjust manner.

Just then they heard a "baaa." Guido had wandered into the stall to steal some of Shady Deal's fresh straw. Dipping his nose down toward Guido, the horse seemed to ease. The goat nibbled at the horse's muzzle and Shady Deal flapped his lips back at the goat.

Punch smiled.

"I just don't get it," Mike said. "Why would someone do this to a horse? I mean, I understand that they were trying to get a point across, but I'd rather they just come after me. At least I'd understand what was happening. This poor guy never will."

He turned his father, who was looking at the horse but not really seeing him. Mike touched his shoulder. "Dad...are you okay?"

"I'm fine. I'm just worried about your sister. I can't stand the not knowing."

"She'll be okay, Eric." Punch let go of Shady Deal and the horse followed Guido around the stall while he was snacking on the horse's hay. "I can't picture Holden hurting her. I can't believe he was helping Walker drug horses. How many trainers do you think were involved?"

"Lugowski said there will be an investigation of the entire racetrack," Eric said. "He imagines there will be at least ten to fifteen trainers brought in on drug charges. He said that Doc ordered extra tests from last night's races and when the results come in there could be even more. That's a dirty rotten shame. The investigation won't stop there. They'll be looking at everyone that works in the test barn, too."

Just then, Eric's cell phone rang. He pulled it from his pocket to look at the screen: Lt. Carl Lugowski. He lifted it to his ear. "What have you got, Lieutenant?"

"We've got a lead, Mr. West," Lugowski said. "Maybe you should come down to the station. You may be able to shed some light on what we plan to do."

* * * * *

Forty-five minutes later, Eric was scouring the map with Jack and Lugowski at the police station.

"He's doing a very good job of staying below the radar," Lugowski reported. "We've got an APB out on Kate's Mustang, but haven't got a single bite. He must be staying off any of the main highways. We checked his bank records. He withdrew three thousand dollars from his account, so he's paying cash for everything they need: food, gas, lodging. We froze his accounts so that if they should come up short, he won't be getting anymore."

"Okay, so you figure they're in Kentucky, but every hour that passes they're moving farther away. What's the plan, gentlemen?" Eric asked.

"We're going to fly into the Cincinnati/ Northern Kentucky Airport," Jack said, "pick up a vehicle and try to follow their route the best we can. We'll have to hope that we get some leads along the way." He looked down at his watch. "The flight doesn't leave until eleven thirty. That's in a little more than two hours."

"I'm going with you," Eric stated.

"I don't think that's possible, Mr. West," Jack said. "We can't be responsible for your safety."

"I don't need you to worry for my safety, Detective Haliday. This is my daughter, and I either come with you or follow you, it makes no difference to me."

Jack opened his mouth to speak, but Lugowski lifted his hand in a halting manner. "Mr. West has ridden shotgun with me before, Jack. He's good to go."

"We're wasting time, gentlemen," Eric said. "Let's get to it."

~ THIRTEEN ~

The candlelight flickered and danced across the oak paneled ceiling to fill the room with a soothing vanilla scent. Mmmm, the bed felt so warm and cozy.

Holden had wrapped his body around Kate like a tight vine. His breathing was deep as he snored softly into her neck. Kate wiggled to get enough room to turn over toward the alarm clock on the nightstand: three p.m.

They had slept for six hours. She wasn't a bit surprised. They had been exhausted from the full day that they'd put in at the racetrack and then the long drive. They still had a long drive ahead of them. Prying her body from underneath his, Kate crawled out of the bed to go to the bathroom.

Holden stirred. Dragging his fingers through his bed-tousled hair, he grumbled when he asked, "What time is it?"

"Three o'clock." She closed the bathroom door.

He pushed to a sitting-up position. The sleep had done him some good, but the dread was waiting patiently for him when he woke.

Shane and the cop were dead by now, their bodies buried deep beneath a dirty horse stall under mats and straw. Chip and his thugs were either carrying on business as usual or they had gotten the hell out of dodge.

It didn't matter. The fact was that there had been two murders and even though he hadn't done the killing, their blood stained his hands just the same.

He scrubbed his fingers across his bristly chin. Kate would be devastated when she found out that Shane was missing. As the days dragged on she would want to go home to be with her family.

He would have to face Eric.

Christ.

Holden dropped his face into his hands. The culpability of knowing Shane's fate scraped through him. Sucking back a sob, he rubbed his eyes furiously with the palms of his hands in an attempt to ward off tears.

The flush of the toilet and the sound of water pouring into the sink brought him to alertness. He stared at the bathroom door. How much longer could he keep Kate in the dark? How much longer could he prevent that inevitable phone call that she'd been insisting to make? He squeezed his eyes closed tightly.

So much to hide.

So many lies to be told.

So much to lose.

"Are you okay?" Kate asked.

Flinching, he looked up. Next to the bed, Kate was eddying into her jeans. He hadn't heard her come out of the bathroom. She pulled up the zipper and buttoned the waistband. She grabbed her backpack from the floor, pulled out a T-shirt and tossed it to him—hitting him in the chest.

With a scandalous curl to her lips, she said, "True confessions: I stole this from your dresser the very first night that I spent at your apartment." She lifted her eyebrows. "Sometimes I sleep in it. But you need a clean shirt, so there you are. What are you going to do for clean underwear, Dr. Reese?"

Holden took in a deep cleansing breath. Licking his lips, he managed an ornery grin for her benefit. "I thought I'd just turn these inside out."

On cue, her expression changed from calm to abhorrence.

He chuckled at the predicted reaction that he evoked from his fiancé. With a shrug he said, "Oh okay, I'll go commando, then."

Crossing her arms under her breasts, Kate threw him a baleful look. "I think we should stop at a store and buy you some necessities: underwear, socks, deodorant, and a razor should be on the list as well. I can't believe you wouldn't take the time to stop at your apartment before we left. You can't go into an interview looking or smelling like a mountain man."

"I'm *your* mountain man."

"Not for long, bucko!" Kate told him in no uncertain terms. "Get in there and get washed up, we're heading for the first Walmart we can find."

Holden clambered out of the bed. "Does that mean I can go commando until we get to Walmart?"

Cupping her hand over her mouth, Kate giggled while she watched his naked body amble toward the bathroom. Lord have mercy—the man had a sinfully fantastic butt.

* * * * *

Only one table remained empty in the dining room when Kate and Holden made their way downstairs to check out. The breakfast they had in the morning had been so delicious that they decided to have dinner before pressing onward. Holden had Kate take a seat, while he did a last check of their room to make sure they hadn't left anything behind. He was relieved when she didn't argue. Rather, she began to peruse the menu.

Holden rushed back to the room to retrieve the gun from the armoire where he'd hidden it. After stuffing it into his jacket, he took a calming breath and then purposefully slowed his movements as he returned to the dining room.

Kate was starving. She ate every bite of the homemade pot roast, mashed potatoes, and carrot soufflé. Moreover, she couldn't resist the homemade black raspberry pie when the server brought around the dessert tray.

"I can't believe you're not hungry," she said to Holden when the server set the pie in front of her. "You haven't touched a thing."

Holden looked down at the fried chicken, baked potato, and mixed steamed vegetables on his plate. He felt like the flaming knot in his stomach was burning a hole right through his midsection. "I'm not feeling very hungry right now."

Kate lifted her chin with her eyes pressed closed and her lips pursed. "Mmm, mmm, mmm, this pie is to die for." She held up a forkful. "Wanna bite?"

Turning his head away, Holden put his hand up. "No, thanks."

"That chicken looks scrumptious. We'll have the server box it up. Maybe you'll be hungry later."

"Maybe," Holden muttered while scanning the guests sitting in the dining room. They were mostly families and one older couple who were more interested in the text messages on their phones than talking to each other. He turned back to Kate. "We should really get going. It's almost five o'clock."

Kate stuffed the last bite of her pie into her mouth, wiped her hands on the napkin, and grabbed her backpack off the chair. "Don't you want the chicken?"

Holden shook his head no.

She shrugged the backpack over her shoulder. "Let's go."

Clara was sweeping the porch when Kate pushed through the door with Holden at her heels. She looked up from her broom. "Thanks for staying with us, Mr. Redman."

Kate hesitated at the top step. She cocked her head. "His name isn't Redman, its Reese."

The right side of Clara's lip curled at Holden. "Have a safe trip, then."

While Holden urged her down the steps, Kate whispered, "Why did she call you Mr. Redman?"

"She checks in a lot of people, Kate," he explained. "She probably just got my name mixed-up is all." He held the car door open for her.

Lifting a shoulder, Kate slipped into her seat and tossed the backpack into the rear seat. She grabbed the GPS from the dash and turned it on. "Reese and Redman aren't even close. Are you sure she didn't register you under the wrong name or something?"

"What difference does it make? I told her my name was Reese and she wrote down Redman or she registered in a Redman after I came in and got me mixed up with him. What the hell do I care?" Holden snapped at her. "Why are you fussing about it?"

"I'm *not* fussing. I'm just pointing out that it seems weird that she would mistake Reese for Redman. I mean Reese is a more common name than Redman, I would think, wouldn't you?"

"Again, I don't give a rat's ass, just leave it be." Holden dropped into the driver's seat, turned on the ignition, and noticed Kate adjusting the GPS.

"We need to make a left out of here," she said.

Agitation burned through his brain. He felt as though the top of his head would soon explode if Kate didn't stop worrying about which direction they were headed or which was the most direct. He wanted to bed rid of the GPS for fear that they could be tracked. He snatched the device from her hand and tossed it out the window.

"Hey! What the hell are you doing? That's mine!"

"I'll buy you a new one."

"I don't need a new one. Stop the car and get it back!"

"Sit back and enjoy the ride, Kate. I can't stand anymore co-piloting. I'll get us where we need to go." He glanced in the side mirrors. "Besides, it broke into a million pieces when it hit the gravel."

Kate spun in the seat to see her GPS scattered over the gravel. "That was completely unnecessary, Reese!"

"Oh, it was necessary, believe me, it was."

Kate flopped back against her seat as Holden rolled the Mustang down the short driveway and onto the gravel road.

Feeling like an errant child that had just been scolded and severely punished, Kate turned her head to watch the rural scenery pass by. Was that how he would be when they married? She bit down on her lip. He was on her last nerve.

Clara watched them pull away. Only moments after she'd returned to her sweeping, her husband's police cruiser, with the word "Sheriff" painted in bold black print on the side, pulled in from the opposite direction. She set the broom aside to watch him climb out of the vehicle and trudge up the steps onto the porch. He looked tired when he reached the top. He took his hat off and stuffed it under his arm.

"The pot roast is really good tonight, Wayne," she said after kissing his cheek.

"Sounds like a plan." He opened the door for her just as dispatch called through his shoulder radio.

"APB in progress: red Mustang convertible, Pennsylvania license number: WEST dash three. Male suspect Holden Reese, six foot two, brown hair, thirty years old, armed. He may be with a blonde woman, Kate West, five foot six, twenty-six years old. Repeat..."

Clara came to a halt. Her eyes widened and her jaw dropped slightly open. "Good Lord, Wayne, that car and those people just pulled out of this driveway!"

Wayne let the screen door slam shut. "Are you sure?"

"Sure as I'm standing here! He signed the register as Holden Redman. But when they left that blonde woman corrected me. She said his name was Reese. They got in a red Mustang convertible, only the top was up. I'm tellin' ya, it was them. They turned left out of the drive." She stared out the driveway as if she could still see them pulling away. Shaking her head while running her hands up and down her arms, she said, "They were very nice. I guess ya just never know about folks, do ya?"

* * * * *

The flight was only an hour and a half long, but it had been delayed by two hours for a minor repair on the plane. With frustration etched on their faces, and their duffle bags slung over their shoulders, Lugowski, Jack, and Eric waited for the attendant at the car rental counter to order up an SUV for them to use. The way things were looking it was going to take two hours to get a vehicle. The attendant was in no hurry.

Jack's cell phone rang. Fumbling, he pulled the phone from his jacket. "Haliday..." Listening intently, his eyebrows rose. He tapped Lugowski on the shoulder. "You gotta pen and pad?"

Lugowski dug into the pocket inside his jacket before producing exactly what Jack had requested. Wedging the phone between his ear and his shoulder, Jack jotted down information on the pad as it was given to him. "Got it, thanks." He then stuffed the phone back into his pocket.

With a smile on his face, Jack told Lugowski and Eric, "The APB finally got a hit. They stayed at a place called..." He glanced down at the pad, "Gertie's Bed and Breakfast. The captain said from the looks on the map, it's about thirty-five or so miles from here. He gave me the address so we'll punch it into the GPS and be on our way."

"If we ever get a vehicle," Eric muttered while tossing a steely look at the attendant.

~ FOURTEEN ~

The late afternoon sun beaming through the windshield lent warmth to the crisp Kentucky air. Driving along the two lanes made the ride more peaceful and scenic. Yet, Kate kept pointing out that the round-about route was going to take them a month of Sundays to get to Houston. After all they were on two lanes rather than interstates. With or without the GPS, she was aware that they couldn't possibly be traveling in the most efficient direction.

Laughing it off, Holden suggested that she relax and take in the countryside. They had plenty of time. After several hours, Kate insisted that they stop to use the restroom. Holden continued driving until dusk draped its purple haze over them, and they came to a secluded stretch of road.

"I just saw a sign that said if you get on the interstate which is just up the road a ways, there's a rest area off the first exit," Kate pointed out.

Holden wasn't in favor of getting on the interstate for even a few miles, but if he didn't Kate would get very upset. "Good, we'll stop there."

"You'd better, or this seat is going to be very soggy," Kate warned.

Holden chuckled at her crossed legs and the straining look on her face when he rolled the Mustang up the entrance ramp to the freeway.

They drove along the interstate for a mere two miles when they came upon the exit that Kate had pointed out. The rest area was snuggled in a remote wooded area. The small block building was corralled in ponderosa pines. Several weathered picnic tables dotted the landscape and the parking lot pavement was cracked and slightly heaved.

Holden was happy to find that no one was about. Kate eyed up the isolated restroom. The dusk-to-dawn lights were blinking into a weary glow, which gave the place an eerie quality while the dusk gave way to dark.

"I thought you had to go," Holden said to pull her from her examination.

"Do you think it's open?"

"Sure, these places are open twenty-four-seven for the truckers. It looks clean, just not used all that much." He gauged her hesitation. "You'd better go,

Kate. I don't think there's another one for a good forty miles or so."

Shouldering the door open, she let out a huffy breath. "We should've stopped at the BP station thirty miles back like I suggested. We could've got snacks there."

"Are you hungry?"

"I could eat. You've got to be starving. You didn't have any dinner."

The knot in Holden's stomach had eased up during the drive. He managed to direct his thoughts to the road, Kate's light conversation, and the country music softly filtering from the radio. Slightly more relaxed than when he woke in the bed and dinner, he did notice a twinge of hunger rumbling in his stomach. "Maybe they'll have some snack machines inside," he said as he followed her up the sidewalk.

"Oh, yummy."

"You're not going all high maintenance on me, are you?"

"Seriously?" she said over her shoulder while yanking the door open.

They stepped inside to find three snack machines lined against the wall along with a rack of maps and sight-seeing brochures below a portrait of the governor of Kentucky. Teasing, Holden pointed at the snack machines with a "voila" expression on his face.

Kate rolled her eyes at him while stepping into the ladies room. Taking a few moments to check out what the machines had to offer, which wasn't much, Holden decided that he'd better make a pit-stop as well.

He meandered into the men's room.

* * * * *

Officer Wells had had one too many cups of coffee in the past three hours. He knew that there was a rest area only a short distance up the highway. The rest area was located in a rather secluded area, so it wasn't a bad idea to stop in to make sure that it was secure.

He steered his cruiser onto the winding entrance ramp toward the rest stop when he noticed the red convertible Mustang parked in a space at the end of the sidewalk. His eyes narrowed. He slowed the cruiser down to take a good look at the license plate: Pennsylvania, WEST- 3.

Yep, he knew that an APB had been issued on this vehicle. His son's girlfriend drove a red convertible Mustang, but very few people had license numbers like that. He dimmed his headlights down to the parking lights, and rolled the cruiser to a stop next to the Mustang.

He picked up the radio. "Officer Wells to dispatch..."

"Go ahead, Officer," the voice filtered through.

"Red Mustang, Pennsylvania license, WEST dash three located at rest area number twenty-two off Route 330."

"Backup on its way, Officer Wells."

He put the radio back in place. Knowing that back-up could be as much as fifteen miles away, he decided to walk into the restroom to try to apprehend the suspect on a casual level. Keeping his eyes on the door, he made his way up the sidewalk, peered through the glass doors, and stepped inside.

The lobby was empty. He heard a toilet flush in the men's room. Drawing his gun, he eased the door open. Through the small gap, he could see Holden washing his hands at the sink. With his gun trained on Holden, Officer Wells stepped into the room and let the door close behind him.

Holden immediately saw the officer in the mirror. He froze at the sight of him holding a gun.

"Holden Reese...put your hands on top of your head," the officer instructed.

Holden's chest tightened. His breathing stopped. They knew about the murders! What the hell did Chip do? It was obvious: Chip told the police that he was in on it! Panic rolled through him like white water in a fast stream. He was going to prison! He couldn't breath. He had to do something.

The officer reached for the handcuffs attached to his belt and for a nanosecond, his gaze dropped to the cuffs. Holden whipped around to slam the officer in the eye with the point of his elbow.

Officer Wells stumbled backwards. Holden smacked the gun from his hand and punched him in the jaw. The officer fell against the bathroom wall. Holden grabbed him by the neck, yanked him the short distance across the room and smacked his face into the sink. Blood splattered over the white porcelain when his head jerked backward and his body fell to the floor—lifeless.

Holden could barely catch his breath. His face was flushed with sweat and panic. The sweat dribbled into his eyes. He swiped his burning eyes with the back of his hand while trying to focus on the officer lying in blood on the floor. Slowly, he knelt next to him and pressed his fingers against his throat.

Officer Wells was dead.

Hiccups of sobs jerking from his chest, Holden backed away from the body. Bile rose in his throat. He rushed to the sink and retched violently. He leaned against the wall. His chest heaved up and down with his heavy breaths. Slowly, he slid down to the floor.

What now?

Terror churned inside him. He was screwed.

Kate! Kate was in the ladies room. He had to get her out of there! He clawed at the wall to clamber to his feet. Quickly, he splashed water over his face, and rinsed his mouth out. As he placed his hands on the door, he took one last look at the dead policeman lying in his own blood on the restroom floor.

* * * * *

As Kate fastened her jeans, she could hear muffled voices coming from the men's room.

Holden was right. This rest area must get some traffic after all. While washing her hands in the sink, she heard a hard thump on the other side of the wall. Her head jerked up and her eyes flicked around the room while she listened.

Hearing nothing more, she turned on the hand dryer. It rattled and vibrated against the wall so loudly that it could have woke the dead.

* * * * *

Holden looked down at the name tag on the officer's shirt: Robert Wells. Now there were three murders: Shane West, the undercover cop, and the police officer...Officer Wells.

He pushed through the door into the lobby.

Kate was studying the assortment of stale candy bars, potato chips, packaged cupcakes, and gum. He palmed her elbow to swiftly lead her to the door.

"Let's go, Kate," he snapped. He practically shoved her across the room and out the door.

"Hey, there's a police cruiser here." She pointed to the end of the sidewalk.

223

"Yep, even cops have to go to the bathroom," Holden groused.

They could hear the muffled voice of the dispatcher coming from the inside of the cruiser when he yanked her door open and pushed her toward the seat. He jogged to the driver's side, dropped into the seat and fired up the engine.

Kate looked across the cab. The dusk-to-dawn lights filtered through the windshield glimmering off the beads of sweat on Holden's face. "You're sweating again. Are you sure you're all right?"

"I'm fine, Kate!" Holden bellowed. "Will you stop your damned fussing?" He had a white knuckle grip on the steering wheel. The tires squealed as he pulled away from the rest stop—ferociously.

Kate was thrown back into her seat. She grabbed the door handle with one hand, and the console with her other.

What had rattled his cage?

They sped down the ramp and back onto the interstate. In the distance, they could hear sirens. Holden sped down the highway until he came to the next exit ramp only to get back onto the interstate going the opposite direction so they could return to the two lane road they had been driving along.

"Did something go on between you and the cop in the bathroom?" Kate asked quietly.

Angrily, Holden replied, "Why would you ask me that?"

"You were fine when you went in, and now you acting like an ass, that's why," she snapped back.

He had to tell her something. He had to pull it together. Holden shook his head. Through a clenched jaw, he said, "He was a real dick. He said I was parked crooked in the space and he was gonna give me a ticket." He spewed a nervous chuckle. "I mean, what difference did it make? There was no one at the freakin' rest stop but us." Lifting his shoulder, he wiped his cheek with his sleeve. "He was the kind of cop who liked to bully people who were minding their own business."

Kate's brows furrowed. "How'd you get out of it?"

"I...um...I just apologized and told him I'd be more careful next time." He ran his nervous fingers through his hair. "He said that I'd better, and then he went into a stall to do his thing. Whatta jerk."

"Oh...I...I...I heard a big bang coming from the men's room, like somebody dropped something."

Holden took in a braced breath. "Yeah, the asshole fell in some water on the floor. He hurt his shoulder. I...um took a quick look at for him. He's okay."

Sinking her teeth into her bottom lip, Kate laid her head against the headrest to watch Holden drive.

His fingers were wrapped so tightly around the steering wheel that it seemed his knuckles could break through the skin at any moment, and he stared through the windshield so fiercely that she thought it would shatter.

"Are you sure that's all that went on? You seem awfully upset."

"What the hell, Kate?" Holden yelled. "Why do you have to question everything I fucking say?"

Surprised at his cursing at her, Kate blinked back. "You don't have to be so nasty! I'm just making sure that you're okay."

"No, it seems like you're accusing me of lying to you! I beat the officer to a bloody pulp! Does that make you feel better?" Holden bit out.

The heat of his anger vibrated through the car to suck out the oxygen. Every muscle in his neck and shoulders seemed to be bunching into tight balls.

"Now you're acting like a total asshole, Holden!" Kate said. "Let's just not talk at all for a while, huh?" With that, she wrapped her arms around herself. She wished she could find her cell phone to call home. At least, if she'd brought along a book, she could escape into another place and time.

She adored Holden, only his moods seemed to swing like that of a pendulum from one extreme to the other.

When the arm of the pendulum swung toward fun easy-going Holden, he was a dream come true. He was a man that every girl would want to be with: handsome, charming, fun, athletic, and oh-so yummy in bed. Ahhh, but when the pendulum was pitched to the other side, he could be as malicious as an agitated Pit Bull.

It seemed that the pendulum was favoring the Pit Bull once more.

The silence stretched between them and although time had stretched as well, Holden's demeanor had not lightened up. The incident in the men's room with the cop had brought out the Holden she hated to deal with. In the confined space of the car, his frame of mind was growing to larger than life proportions.

Kate decided to do the only thing that was available: stare out the window, give him space, and hopefully he'd cool off. Yet, every time she dared a peek, he seemed more explosive.

Finally, he said, "Kate..."

She turned. She could see that he was struggling. His lips quivered like he was trying to suppress emotional words that were bubbling to the surface against his will. He swallowed a thick slug of salvia, and then his hand reached out for hers. Kate took his hand. It was clammy.

"I'm sorry for what I said to you back there. I don't ever want to hurt you." He bit his lip, like he was trying to control each word that tumbled from his mouth. "I promise, once we get to Texas everything will be more settled. We'll have left everything behind, and it will be just you and me. No more distractions."

What was he talking about? We'll have left everything behind? What was it that they needed to leave behind? The affair that he'd had with Ava? Kate thought that they'd worked that out months ago. They had left it behind. They were engaged. It all seemed to be working out.

Was it her family? His word from the other day rang loudly in her ears, "Everyone's always up in our business." Okay, maybe they were, but it wasn't enough for them to make a mad dash for Texas like two outlaws on the run.

Kate offered him with a feeble smile. She leaned back against the seat and returned to staring out into the darkness.

Quite frankly, she was really getting tired of Holden's moody bullshit.

~ FIFTEEN ~

As dusk was taking hold, Lugowski, Jack, and Eric climbed out of the rented Ford Explorer at Gertie's Bed and Breakfast. The air had grown cooler toward evening and the scent of Sassafras was bolder.

Several guests from the B&B were rocking to and fro on the chairs on the porch. They were laughing and chatting when the three men climbed the steps.

Sheriff Wayne Knots greeted them at the door. "Come on in, boys. I assume you're from the Rosemount Police Department?"

Lugowski nodded.

Wayne directed them to a table in the empty dining area where Clara was sitting with her fingers wrapped around a cup of tea. "We can talk over here," the sheriff said. "Clara doesn't want the guests to know that anything is going on...it's bad for business, you understand."

Lugowski asked, "How is she explaining your presence?"

"Oh, I'm here a lot. I'm her husband." He offered his hand to Lugowski, "I'm Wayne Knots, the sheriff in this county. I'm usually referred to as the Sheriff of Nottingham." He laughed and they all politely chuckled along with him. Wayne continued, "This is my wife, Clara. She runs this bed and breakfast."

Jack introduced the group. "I'm Detective Jack Haliday. This is Lieutenant Carl Lugowski, and Eric West."

Wayne shook hands with the men, as did Clara. Then, they all pulled up chairs to the table. A server brought out a tray of cups and a carafe filled with hot coffee. There was silence at the table until the server returned to the kitchen.

Finally, Jack pulled out two photographs and laid them on the table in front of Clara. "Are these the two individuals that stayed here?"

Clara examined the photos. She lifted her gaze to meet Jack's. With a nod, she said, "Yes, this young man checked in as Holden Redman, but this young lady..." She pointed at the photograph of Kate. "corrected me as they were leaving—said his name was Holden Reese. They drove away in a red Mustang convertible."

"How long did they stay?" Jack asked.

"Only for the day," she answered. "The man said that they only needed to get some rest—they'd been driving all night. They looked very tired when they checked in. They came downstairs around four o'clock and had dinner here, and then they left. They seemed very nice."

"Did the young lady seem like she was with Mr. Reese by choice?" Eric asked.

Clara measured Eric for a moment. She could see the concern in his face. "Oh yes, they seemed like a young couple in love," she said. "Only I must say she didn't seem nearly as...uptight as he did. He seemed nervous. I guess that's why he didn't want to give me his right name. At first, I thought it might be an affair situation. He paid cash for everything. I guess I know why now. Anyway, they turned left out of the driveway."

"They must be heading for the freeway—" Wayne said, and then he was interrupted by his shoulder radio.

The dispatcher announced, "Officer found dead at rest stop number twenty-two, Route 330. Officer called in the pending APB before entering the building."

Exchanging wary glances, everyone at the table froze.

Crestfallen, Eric was the first to put it into words. "Holden has killed a police officer. This ups the ante."

"Yes, it does, Mr. West," Jack said, "It could mean that your daughter is an accessory to murder."

Clara grabbed her chest. "That girl was your daughter?"

Eric's steely gaze never left Jack's as he replied to Clara's question, "Yes, ma'am, she is, and Kate would never participate willingly in a murder. Not for anyone, and that includes Holden."

Closing his eyes, Lugowski rubbed his forehead. "Do you have a map, Sheriff?"

"Sure do." Wayne made his way to the registration desk, opened a cabinet, and then returned to spread a map across the table. He pointed to the area where the officer had been found. "This is Route 330, and this is approximately where that rest station is. That's a good forty-five to fifty miles from here. Looks like they're heading for the Tennessee line, but they sure aren't going the most direct route." He slid his finger across the map to a long red line. "They should've taken this road...Interstate 264."

Jack and Eric's tense moment was set aside while they both studied the map.

"Looks to me like he's avoiding the interstates," Lugowski said. "He's taking all the two lanes—

trying to duck any police. Do you mind if we take this with us?"

"You're welcome to it, Lieutenant."

Just then a young boy came running into the dining area. He came to the table with a smashed device in his hand. "I found this in the driveway. My dad said I had to bring it in," he explained as he handed it to Clara.

"Thank you," she said.

The boy hurried back outside.

Clara handed the device to Lugowski.

"Well, it was a GPS," he said. "Now, it's a piece of junk."

Eric took it from Lugowski. "This was Kate's. I bought it for her for Christmas several years ago when she was planning a trip out west."

"Well whatta ya know," Jack said, "she did have a GPS."

"And Holden knew we could track it so he got rid of it," Lugowski said. "Things could be escalating, gentlemen."

* * * * *

The skin rippled over the bone of Holden's clenched jaw. His grip hadn't loosened on the steering wheel, and he was driving way over the speed limit.

Kate bit her tongue. She feared that any reprimand or word of caution from her would surely result in a major melt-down, which looked well under-way as it was. She certainly didn't care to have another verbal altercation.

Instead, she made sure her seatbelt was secure and kept a good hold on the door handle with her right hand and the center console with her left. Mechanically, her right foot pressed on an imaginary brake peddle when they rounded a bend.

Finally, Holden turned to her. "I need to regroup. I'm still very tired. Do you mind if we stop for the night?"

Kate let out a relieved breath. "I'm feeling pretty beat myself. That might be a good idea. I saw a sign about a mile back that said there was a hotel coming up soon."

Holden seemed detached from the decision even though he responded with a nod.

Kate would be thankful to put her feet to the ground outside of the car. Maybe he hadn't had enough rest. She'd never seen him quite this fretful. He was beside himself in a way she couldn't put into words. He needed to calm down.

It was tearing her apart, but Kate was reconsidering the matter of setting a wedding date.

He turned the car off the two lane onto another road, which appeared quite remote. Kate couldn't imagine that there would be any major hotel chains on this stretch of road, and she was right. As they weaved down the road, a motel came into view.

It was a two-story motel with rooms on both levels. The vertical neon sign reminded her of something one would see in an old movie. A large arrow pointed toward the building with the words: Blue Moon Motel. The "n" was burned out, and the letter "e" in the word "motel" was blinking like it would be the next victim.

Kate thought it resembled a hideout for bank robbers, kidnappers, drug dealers, and the like.

The Blue Moon Motel definitely would not appear on any magazine's "best destination" lists.

There was another neon sign that hung crooked in the office window that blinked with the word: Vacancies.

No surprises there.

The Mustang bumped over heaved pavement, and dipped into the potholes that plagued the parking lot. Drawing closer, they could see the poor condition of the place. Kate could only imagine that they probably had bedbugs...or worse.

Pulling into a spot in front of the office and turning off the ignition, Holden took in the less than upscale motel. He let out a sigh. "Well, it ain't the Ritz would be an understatement." He shouldered the door open. "But we should be able to get some rest, anyway."

"I doubt it," Kate murmured to herself when Holden slammed the car door closed. She watched him make his way to the office.

He emerged from the office a few minutes later with a room key dangling in his hand. Kate couldn't believe it. It was an actual key—not a swipe card—a key. Oh, yeah this place was really up to snuff.

They had only taken a few steps toward the building when Holden turned to Kate. "Oh, could you get the bags from Walmart? I want to shave and put on some clean boxers. I'll open the room."

"What room number?"

"We're in twelve—up the stairs, second room in."

"I'll be up in a minute."

Holden trotted up the cement stairs that was hidden between two walls to make his way to the top floor. He found the room and pushed the key into the lock and stepped inside. Slapping the switch, the room was flooded with light to reveal its old décor, dingy walls, and faded gold bed spread. The thick drapes hung above the single pained window's sills. He grabbed the cord to yank them closed. Then, he hurried across the room to pull the telephone from the wall and tossed it under the bed.

He heard the rollers on Kate's small suitcase bumping along the cement floor outside. Her backpack only held so much. She must've decided to reload from the things that she'd shoved into the case.

Holden felt a pang of shame when Kate stepped into the room. She was dragging her suitcase. Her backpack was shrugged over her shoulder, while

236

two Walmart bags dangled from her right forearm. Moreover, she looked done in and stressed out. He should have helped up bring the load up, but then he wouldn't have been able to get to the room before her. He watched her gauge the room. Dissatisfaction snaked across her face. Her lips pursed. Her nose crinkled.

"I know, I know, it isn't exactly the Taj Mahal—"

"Taj Mahal? It doesn't even equal the Red Roof," Kate said.

Her eyes measured the carpeting. There was a ground-in dirt path from the door to the bathroom. The scarred furniture had once been of the French provincial style, but now was nothing more than drab somewhat white furnishings. The bathroom door was warped and cracked. Kate wasn't sure that she even wanted to know what the shower or toilet looked like.

"I hope you didn't pay too much for this dump." Kate dropped the Walmart bags to the floor.

"Forty bucks."

"They should be paying us as far as I'm concerned." Kate heaved the suitcase onto the bed. Her lip wrinkled at the sight of the bedspread. "I hope they at least changed the sheets since the last guests stayed in this room."

"They have to. It's the law." Holden fought to hold back his agitation.

"Yeah...and everything on the internet is the gospel truth."

Holden understood her unease. He opened his arms, "Come here."

Rolling her eyes, Kate went to his embrace. He swallowed her into his chest and rested his cheek on top of her head. "It's only for one night. We'll be on our way in the morning—feeling more refreshed."

Kate looked up at him.

His eyes were bruised with fatigue mixed with angst. She managed a meager smile. "I suppose." Pulling from his arms, she looked to the night-stand. "No telephone? Again? I don't believe it. What's with these hotels?"

"Like I said before: everyone has a cell nowadays, baby."

"Well I don't have a cell. I just can't imagine where it is and I really need to call Dad."

"You left a note."

"Holden...it's going on two days since he's heard from or seen me. He's probably getting a bit jumpy by now, don't you think?"

Holden let out a huff of frustration. "You can call him when we get to Houston."

"Seriously, Holden?"

His cheeks flushed. Taking a deep breath, he kissed her on the forehead and decided to end the conversation before it turned into a war. "I'm going to take a shower, and then we're going to bed. Just kick back and relax, will ya? Stop fussing." With that Holden grabbed the two Walmart bags from the floor and headed for the bathroom.

Sinking onto the bed, Kate trapped her hands between her knees. She took in the shabby motel room while listening to Holden's boots drop with a heavy clunk to the bathroom floor. The water in the shower crashed against the walls.

The room smelled musty with a not-so-subtle hint of cigarette. She needed some fresh air and maybe a little distance from Dr. Holden Reese. She pushed from the bed and stepped out on the walkway overlooking the parking lot. The motel clerk was looking over her Mustang while smoking a cigarette. Keeping her eye on him, she made her way down the dark stairs and walked up behind him.

"Nice car, huh?" Kate said.

He turned. "Yeah, hot."

"I'm staying in room number twelve..."

"Yeah, I know. You're our only check in tonight." Snorting, he added, "You're our only check in for the week."

Right...another big surprise.

"Well, there's a problem with our room. It doesn't have a telephone," Kate said as if that were the only thing wrong with the room.

Narrowing his eyes, the clerk cocked his head to one side. "It doesn't? It should have one. All the rooms should have a phone." He shook his head. "It's amazing what people will steal. I'm sorry about that. C'mon in the office. You can use our phone."

The clerk tossed his cigarette to the pavement and smashed it with his heel. She followed him into the small office, which had the same musty/cigarette smell as their room. The décor wasn't much improved either. The registration counter was in need of a good sanding and fresh paint, but they had a telephone and that was all Kate cared about.

The clerk lifted the phone within her reach.

"Thank you." She lifted the receiver to her ear and dialed her home phone at Westwood. The phone rang and rang.

Biting her lip, Kate hung up. "There was no answer, may I try another number?"

"Go right ahead," the clerk said.

This time Kate dialed her father's cell phone.

~ SIXTEEN ~

Stewing, Eric sat in the backseat of the SUV. There were certain things in this life that he was absolutely positive of: the sun would rise in the morning, the moon would shine at night, and his daughter would not participate in a murder.

Holden was on the run. After the encounter with the police officer at the rest area, he knew that the police were after him. Where did that leave Kate? The woman from the B&B claimed that they seemed like a young couple in love. Kate did not appear to be in distress, but Holden did—that was before Holden bumped into the officer at the rest area. Somehow Holden was hiding the dire situation from Kate. Nonetheless, how did he manage to kill a police officer without her knowing? Or did he?

He dragged his fingers through his hair, leaned his head back, and closed his eyes.

If Kate had witnessed the murder, what was her relationship with Holden now? Had she become his hostage or was she playing along with him until she could get help? He let out a long breath. Lord in Heaven, he'd give anything to be sitting around the dining room table with his entire family while Jen fussed over what wine to serve with her pork roast.

While Jack drove through the darkness, Lugowski studied the map that Wayne had given him under the map light. Mechanically, his hand would wander to the pocket inside his jacket to finger the pack of cigarettes that he yearned to crack open and smoke.

Lugowski agreed with Eric completely: Kate would not condone a murder.

When this hot mess began, Lugowski was certain that Holden would not harm Kate. Now? All bets were off. Holden Reese knew he was being pursued. People on the run usually became desperate and unreliable. Holden had already acted out violently.

Lugowski could only pray that the violence wouldn't bleed into Kate's direction.

He glanced across the cab at Jack Haliday—the lucky one inside the vehicle. He wasn't as close to the situation. He wasn't Kate's father, nor was he a man who had deep unresolved feelings for her.

The feelings Lugowski had were confusing and they scared the hell of him. Yet he could see the contemplation in Jack's expression and posture as he drove along the two lane roads. Lugowski knew that Jack was motivated by the same objective as the two invested men in the SUV: bring Kate home—safe and sound.

The silence in the vehicle was broken by the sound of Eric's cell phone ringing. Thinking it was most likely Jen or Mike or Shane, Eric casually pulled the phone from his pocket and looked at the screen: UNKNOWN NUMBER.

Eric brought the phone to his ear. "Hello..."

"Hi, Dad..."

Relief to hear his daughter's voice washed over him. Cupping his hand over the phone, he whispered to his fellow passengers, "It's Kate!"

Lugowski twisted in his seat. "Don't tell her anything!" he ordered in a low voice. "Let her tell you, and don't tell her that we're following them."

Eric nodded his agreement with Lugowski's instructions. He pressed the button for the speaker phone so that Jack and Lugowski could hear her remarks.

With measured words, Eric said, "I haven't heard from you in a couple days, I was getting worried. How are you?"

243

"I'm really sorry about that. I've lost my cell phone. Didn't you find my note?" Eric exchanged speaking glances with Lugowski.

Jack's eyes flicked to the rearview mirror.

Eric remembered thinking it strange that Kate wouldn't leave him a note. Evidently she did, and evidently Holden had disposed of it.

"No ..." Eric replied. "Like I said, I was getting worried."

"Oh ... Holden has a job interview at Lone Star, so we're on our way there. I don't know why, but Holden sure is taking the scenic route. He seems so out of sorts, maybe he's having second thoughts about the interview." Kate tangled the phone cord around her finger. She glanced furtively over her shoulder toward the office door. "I called home, where are you?"

Eric hesitated. He exchanged looks with Lugowski, and then he said, "Ooh, Jen and I decided to take a drive for some ice cream."

"Tell Jen I said hi," Kate said with a crack in her voice. How she wished she could talk to Jen about what was going on with Holden, but she couldn't spend that much time on the phone and she didn't want to upset her father.

Kate's mention of Jen urged a smile from Eric. He knew that the two of them had grown close. Kate seemed hesitant.

No longer able to resist, he asked, "Sooo, are you almost to Houston or are you in for the night?"

"We're at a little motel called the Blue Moon...I'm not sure, but I think we might be in Tennessee."

Lugowski yanked his cell phone from his pocket and tapped the name of the motel into Google search.

Kate continued, "It's in the middle of nowhere. Holden was very tired and very cranky so we stopped for the night. Hey, how's Shady Deal?"

"He's coming along slowly. We sure could've used Holden, but Doc Spears came out to check on him." He could hear a sense of loss in her voice. He had to know. In an easy voice, he asked, "Is everything okay, Kate?"

She took in a ragged breath. No, everything was not okay. Holden's mood swings were getting the best of her. He had never been so terse with her before. He'd never cursed at her like he had just hours ago, and the way he had purposely broke her GPS was unnerving.

Tears burst from her eyes and her lips quivered as she admitted, "Not really, Dad. I...I just don't know about Holden anymore. I love him, I really do, but I just don't know if I can marry him..."

Eric's entire body tensed.

When the headlights from a passing car swept over Jack's face, Eric could see his eyes narrow in the rearview mirror.

Lugowski paused in his search for the motel. He felt like his heart had just dropped to his stomach.

"Sometimes he's so fun-loving and charming," she said, " and then without warning he turns into some sort of Mr. Hyde." A hiccup of a sob escaped before she could suck it back. "I don't know if I can deal with this on a forever basis. I don't know if I can or if I want to marry Holden." She wiped her nose with the back of her hand.

From behind the counter, the clerk offered her a tissue. She accepted it with an wobbly smile.

Eric took in a deep breath. His daughter was troubled and he had no real way to console her. "He hasn't hit you or anything, has he?"

"Oh no, it's nothing like that. He just gets all nasty-ass...maybe I'm just overly tired. We've been on the road a lot. I should get back upstairs to the room, he'll be wondering where I am."

Again, the three men exchanged glances with furrowed brows.

Eric asked, "Aren't you calling from your room?"

"No...there's no phone in our room. There wasn't one at the bed and breakfast that we stopped at either. I don't know what's up with that. Anyway, I'll call you when we get to Houston. I love you, Dad."

"I love you too, Kate. Be safe," Eric said, and then the line went dead.

They drove for a mile or so in total silence until finally Lugowski spoke, "Kate knows nothing of the dead cop, or the fact that they're on the run. By the sound of her voice she seems like she knows that something is wrong, but she doesn't know what."

"I agree," Jack said. "We need to get to that motel, and we need back-up."

"I'm sure the locals will accommodate us," Lugowski put in.

"Mmmm," Jack said, "we're a little out of our jurisdiction here, boys—especially after the cop killing."

"Agreed," Lugowski said.

"I was thinkin' we'd need backup that is a little more convincing." Jack hitched his chin toward Lugowski's cell phone. "Get Lutz on the line, dude."

* * * * *

Under the hot spray in the shower, Holden hoped the water would wash away the guilt, the remorse, and the anxiety. He bowed his head and let the water stream over his hair and down his face until it finally ran cool. Turning the water off, he grabbed a towel and stepped out onto a mat.

He wiped the steam away from the mirror to leave behind a wide swath of moisture. He looked into the mirror at his heavy stubble and menacing expression—the reflection of a murderer.

Shaking the ominous thought from his mind, he directed his attention to the plastic bag lying on the floor filled with personal hygiene products, namely shaving cream and a razor. He lathered up his face to shave away two days worth of growth. When he washed away the excess foam he looked cleaner, more presentable, but no less blameworthy than before.

The very idea of Shane West's body rotting under a horse's stall made his legs unsteady. Feeling queasy, he closed the lid on the toilet and sat down.

Officer Wells' body lying on the floor of the men's room bled into his minds eye.

Holden stared at the cracked and discolored tile floor beneath his feet without really seeing it. He dropped his elbows to his knees and buried his face into his hands.

Having no control over it, the sobs burst from his throat.

What a mess this whole nightmare had become—worse than he could have ever imagined.

* * * * *

When Kate crept through the door Holden was just coming out the bathroom in his boxer briefs. He looked at her with accusation in his eyes that she couldn't decipher. He cocked his head to the side and furrowed his brows. "Where did you go?" he asked in a clipped tone that signaled that his mood had not lightened.

Kate measured him for a moment. "I went...I was just outside the door. I...wanted some fresh air. And...I wanted to see if our car was still the only one in the parking lot."

Holden quickened to the window to pinch back the dusty curtains. He looked down to the poorly lit parking area. "Is it?" He realized that he couldn't see the car from that angle anyway.

"I don't think many people stay at this motel, Holden."

Letting the curtain drop back into place, he muttered, "I suppose."

Kate grabbed some fresh underwear, her satin pajama pants, and a pair of slippers from her suitcase. "I'm going to take a shower. I won't be long."

After Kate retired into the bathroom, Holden placed her suitcase on the dresser and then pulled down the blankets. He slid into the bed and laced his fingers together behind his head. His body went limp with exhaustion while he watched a spider crawl along the ceiling. He tried not to think about Shane's death or the fact that Kate would soon find out that her brother was missing.

Without invitation, the cop in the rest area invaded his thoughts. He didn't mean to kill him. He just wanted to render him unconscious so that he and Kate could leave undetected.

Holden squeezed his eyes closed.

He could see the blood on the floor at the rest stop. The cop's crushed nose and cheek. Officer Wells looked to be late forties, possibly fifty. He probably had a wife—maybe some kids. He wouldn't be going home to them tonight.

How did this get so fucked up?

~ SEVENTEEN ~

Pointing to a stall, Kate called to Holden, "Holden! Hurry!"

A bright light splashed into the darkness of the barn aisle from within the stall. Kate was beside herself with panic. Her face was flushed and wet with tears. He ran down the long narrow aisle yet his legs felt as heavy as fifty pound blocks. She seemed so far away and the light from the stall beamed like a beacon rendering her a dark silhouette in the backsplash. When he arrived at the entrance of the stall, Kate faded away. He couldn't find her anywhere.

"Kate...Kate..." Holden called after her as he stepped into the brightness of the stall. The tall bay Thoroughbred, Shady Deal, stood swaggering back and forth on wobbly legs. Blood dripped from his head, down his chest, and into the luminous straw beneath his hooves. The straw gleamed like strands of gold. The

blood from the horse beaded against the straw sparkling like rubies.

A familiar voice called from under the straw, "Please! Don't let them kill us!" Shane pleaded. Suddenly, bloodied hands reached through the straw to grasp Holden's feet. Shane's voice grew louder—desperate. His face appeared just below the strands of glimmering straw. His once handsome features were battered and caked with mud. He pleaded, "Holden, help us! We've done nothing wrong! We don't deserve to die!"

Holden fell against the wall in an attempt to turn and run. He clawed at the wall to get up.

Chip Walker stepped into the brilliance. His dark hair shone in the light. He looked into Holden's eyes with disdain. "Where've you been?" he demanded. "We've got new clients. I need scripts. Parker is with Kate. He's going to hurt her if you don't give me scripts. Do you hear me, Doc?" He bellowed while reaching his greedy hand out to him.

Holden's throat tightened. He couldn't breathe. He shoved Chip aside to stumble into the long dark aisle. Shane's voice followed him while he ran to the barn door that seemed to grow miles away with every step he took.

The floor was giving under his harried footsteps. He barely made it to the door when it gave way and the stable fell into a deep funnel.

Holden scrambled into the roadway between the shed rows. He jumped into his truck. He had to get *away. He had to find Kate so they could go somewhere to have a life together.*

"Are you a man of integrity, Dr. Reese?" Eric West's words banged in his ears over and over again.

Desperation churned in his chest. His throat was dry and scratchy. He tried to call Kate's name, but no words would come out.

Turning the key, he shoved the truck into gear to drive erratically through the shed rows. Out of the blue, a young woman stepped from behind one of the manure bins. He slammed his foot to the brake. The truck slid to crash into her. He opened his mouth to scream, but nothing came out.

Quickly, he shouldered the door open. He slowed down as he slid from the seat and with measured steps he made his way to the front of the truck.

Only it wasn't the young woman who lay under the front tires—rather Officer Wells. His face was crushed, and his eyes were closed.

Leaning against the truck, Holden tried to catch his breath.

Suddenly the officer's eyes jerked open and he spoke, but it wasn't the officer's voice that came out of his mouth. It was Shane's. "You killed me, and you're going to pay!"

Holden sat bolt up in the bed, "Bahhhh!" he screamed.

His body was covered in a thick layer of sweat. Desperation gripped his chest, while trepidation grabbed him by the throat. He searched the room to find Kate draped over the chair next to the bed. She was looking at him like he had lost his mind. She wasn't too far off the mark.

"What's going on with you, Holden?" Only she didn't ask in a tender, caring way—it was more of a demand filled with frustration.

He dragged his fingers through his sweaty hair to push it from his face. "I had a bad dream, is all."

"Yeah, no shit." Kate moved from the chair to edge of the bed. "You've been thrashing in that bed for over a half hour. You've been out of sorts since we left that rest area. Now, what the hell is wrong with you? I can't help but think that something other than a misunderstanding over a parking spot went on between you and that cop."

Without warning he grabbed her by the shoulders and slammed her against the mattress so hard that her slippers flipped from her feet. He held her there while she struggled beneath him.

"Stop it!" Kate yelled.

"Stop pushing at me!" he shouted back while bouncing her against the mattress with every syllable. "Stop fussing at me! Just lay still and go to sleep. I need quiet, and I need you to be still!"

Kate stopped struggling. She could see the torment in his eyes. It was almost as though it was no longer Holden that she was looking at. He had taken on a new persona—someone that she didn't recognize. He was pressing down on her so hard that she feared he'd break her collar bones.

This was the moment—this was the instant that she realized that something was more than desperately wrong. She didn't know what it was, and she knew that this was not the time to push.

Submitting, she lay completely still and allowed her breathing to calm in hopes that he would do the same.

He held her there for a while longer—his tortured gaze burning into hers. Droplets of sweat fell from his hair onto the pillow until he finally rolled off her body. He ran his fingers through her hair. She could feel him trying to cool down—trying to come to grips with whatever was so very wrong.

Finally, he spoke. His words were raspy and quiet, yet concise. "I'm sorry. Just let me hold you, and I'll feel better soon." With that, he wrapped himself around her as he had done at the bed and breakfast—like a vine entangled in a trellis.

As she lay there in the dark listening to the rumble and the click and then the grate rattle to a high pitched whirr of the old furnace pushing warm air into the room, Kate tried to work out exactly when it all went to hell. Holden had his tense moods before they had arrived at Gertie's, but his disposition really went over the line after the encounter with the cop at the rest station. She remembered the loud bang coming from the men's room while she was washing her hands. Did the altercation with the cop become physical? Why? Holden wasn't a criminal. They were only using the rest rooms like anyone else. Did Holden injure the cop? How badly?

Kate was unnerved by Holden's outburst and physical backlash. Oftentimes, she felt like she was walking on the proverbial egg shells when she was with him. That feeling was escalating as each day past. She simply didn't want to deal with it anymore.

Finally, she made a decision: when they arrived at Lone Star, she was going to drive home. She needed time and space to think about her future with Holden—if she had a future with him at all.

Even in sleep, he seemed explosive. His brows were furrowed and his mouth was twisted in despair. In the dark, she listened to the sounds of the furnace and his breathing for more than an hour. Holden's body never really relaxed, and her body was cramping from being held in the same position for a long period of time.

Stealthily, she wiggled and crawled out from under his grip until she was able to slip from the bed. The room was dark except for the sliver of moonlight coming through the curtains. Now that she was free from the bed, Kate wasn't exactly sure what she was going to do.

Searching for her slippers, she found the right slipper lying on the floor next to the chair that she'd been sitting in earlier. She snatched it from the floor and pushed her foot into it while continuing her search for the left. Cringing, she realized that she would have to get on the floor to see if it had landed under the bed. Slowly, she knelt next to the bed to peer underneath. Even in the faint light she could see the layers of dust.

She blinked back.

There, amongst the filth, was something else that shook her trust to the core.

~ EIGHTEEN ~

A slice of sunlight peered through the gap in the curtains to sting Holden's eyes. He rolled over to reach for the lovely blonde sleeping next to him. Kate's side of the bed was empty. Groaning while rubbing the sleep from his eyes, he pushed up to his elbow only to find Kate sitting cross-legged on the chair with a scowl on her face.

"Look what I found...under the bed." Accusation vibrated through Kate's tone. She held up the room's telephone for him to see. Her blue eyes scorched with anger.

"What was it doing there?"

"I dunno. Why don't you tell me?"

"How should I know?" Holden plopped back against his pillow.

"Because upon closer inspection, there was an outline in the dust on the nightstand where it apparently always sits." Kate picked up a book from the nightstand. "Just like this Gideon Bible has a dust line around it. Their maid isn't big on attention to detail." She slammed the Bible back into its place. "It was really gross, but I started looking around for my slippers and there it was—among the thick layer of dust bunnies under the bed!"

"Did you call anyone?"

"Why did you hide the phone from me, Holden?"

"Jesus, Kate, what makes you think I hid the phone? It could've been there since the last person that used the room." He tossed the blankets out of the way and threw his legs over the side of the bed. He grabbed his pants from the floor to quickly shrug into them. Reaching for a T-shirt, he said, "I'm going to go pay our bill. Be ready to leave when I get back."

Kate slammed the phone onto the nightstand. "Why?"

"Don't fuss—just get ready, Kate. We need to get on the road. I'd like to be in Houston by tonight."

"Seriously? For someone who's in a big-ass hurry, you sure have been taking the scenic route!"

Holden dashed around the bed, grabbed Kate by the arm, and yanked her from the chair. "I said get ready!" He shoved her toward the bathroom.

Kate's feet became entangled. With a yelp, she fell to the floor. Holden reached to help her up, but she swatted his hand away. "Don't touch me!" she yelled.

Kate had had as much as she was going to take. It was time for Dr. Holden Reese to answer the questions that had been burning inside her all night long. Letting go of all the tension and frustration that she'd been swallowing back, she hollered, "What's wrong with you, Holden? Why are you hiding the phone from me? Did you hide the phone at Gertie's, too? Why are you thrashing in the bed and sweating all the time? What went on between you and that cop? I can't stand your moods anymore! You're like a girl on her a fucking period!"

Holden stood over her, running a harried hand through his hair, looking into her glowering eyes. There was a stiff knock at the door.

From the other side of the door, a voice called, "Doctor Reese, this is Agent Galletta with the FBI. I'm with Lieutenant Lugowski and Detective Haliday from the Rosemount Police Department. We'd like to talk with you, please."

Holden's spine stiffened.

Kate pushed to a sitting-up position.

Holden put his finger to his lips for Kate to be quiet.

She whispered, "Why does the FBI want to talk to you?"

Holden grabbed her by the arm, yanked her to her feet, and shoved her toward the bathroom. "I don't know! Get dressed!"

Grabbing her clothes from the dresser, Kate shuffled toward the bathroom. She stopped to glare at him before closing the door.

Holden slipped into a T-shirt and then rushed to his jacket laying on the TV stand to retrieve the gun from the inside pocket. The rap on the door became hard, more insistent.

"We know you're in there, Dr. Reese," Galletta said, "and we know that Miss West is with you. Please come out so no one gets hurt."

Holden drew closer to the door and called out, "I didn't have anything to do with those murders, agent. So you can be on your way."

Kate flew out of the bathroom in her lace bra. Her jeans weren't zipped. Her face was flushed with irritation and her eyes wide in horror. "What murders? What the hell are they talking about, Holden?" She cupped her hand over her mouth and gasped at the sudden realization that Holden was holding a gun. "What are you doing with a gun?"

"Come out now, Dr. Reese!" Galletta called from outside.

"I've got a gun! I'll use it! Now, I told you, I didn't have anything to do with it!" Holden yelled back. Sweat poured down his reddened face. He glanced at Kate, who was clinging to the bathroom door jamb with a wan expression on her face while trying to come to grips with what was going on. Suddenly, all the answers to all of her questions were right in front of her and it was a damning reality.

* * * * *

The parking lot below was full of police vehicles. Agent Lou Galletta flanked one side of the hotel room door with a SWAT team lined up behind him, while Lugowski and Jack stood on the other side. They were wearing Kevlar vests and had their guns drawn.

"I'd rather negotiate with him for a while before we force our way in. I don't want to get the young woman hurt," Galletta said to Lugowski and Jack.

"I've met Holden several times," Lugowski said. "He's a level-headed guy. I'd think if we let him settle down a bit you should be able to talk him down. Kate is probably trying to talk some sense to him right now. We should give her some room."

Galletta turned to the SWAT team. "Stand down," he told them. "Let's move to the parking lot and get everyone in position, so we can set a plan in motion."

* * * * *

Kate marched toward Holden. "What the hell is going on, Holden? And don't you dare tell me that you don't know!"

Holden was gasping for air. His anxiety level had reached crescendo. He plopped down on the bed. For a moment, he stared at the wall as if he was somewhere else, and then he hung his head and began to sob.

Slowly, Kate eased down next to him. She bent over to look at his face. "What is it, Holden? Who was murdered? The cop at the rest area?"

Holden tried to mouth the words, yet nothing came out. He nodded, and then his voice came out hoarse and morbid. "Oh, yeah, he's dead, too. I didn't mean to kill him. I slammed him against the sink and he died." Holden wiped his nose with the back of his hand. "But I don't think that's who they are talking about—not with Lugowski here."

Kate's heart was in her throat. Her mouth was dry as a bone, but she managed, "There's more? W-who?"

"Oh, God! Oh, God, Kate—Shane! Your brother and Dave Blake, he wasn't a jockey—he was an undercover cop. I'm pretty sure they took out Doc Spears, too."

Kate drew back. Her eyes widened in horror. Inhaling a hard-to-find breath, she rose from the bed. Unable to believe what the man that she had been in love with had just told her that he had killed her brother, she staggered around the room in a daze.

"I had nothing to do with it, Kate! You've got to believe me! It was Chip! Chip Walker!" he cried.

Trying to breathe, Kate backed toward the door. She wanted nothing more than to get as far away from Holden Reese as possible.

Holden jumped up from the bed. Pacing the room like a madman, he explained, "I was writing scripts for Chip. He had a horse drugging ring going at the track. Lots of trainers were involved. I was only supposed to give him a couple scripts and then be done with it, but he wouldn't let me out. I guess Doc Spears found out about it and got the police involved. That's where Dave Blake came in. I don't know what the hell Shane was doing there! Chip shot them and buried them in a stall.

"That's why we needed to leave. So Chip couldn't say I was involved. You believe me, don't you, Kate?" He took a step toward her. "Don't you?"

Kate's eyes were watery and piercing at the same time. The way she was looking at him exacerbated his anxiety. He thought his head would explode.

Then, he noticed her hand on the door knob. She managed to yank the door partially open. Holden dove toward her and slammed the door closed. He shoved Kate against the wall hard. She fell to the floor.

"You can't leave me now!" he squalled.

He thrust the gun into Kate's face. His eyes were crazed and the sweat ran down his face. His T-shirt was soaking up moisture fast.

He didn't even remotely resemble the Holden that she'd fallen in love with. He looked like someone else—someone she'd never met.

After taking a deep breath and swallowing hard, he managed to soften his tone. "Go sit on the bed. I...I need to think."

The gun shook violently in his hand, while he wiped his face with the other shaking hand.

It seemed like her mind had gone numb. The thoughts were so jumbled that none of them would collect into one coherent thought. Mechanically, Kate pushed from the floor and made her way to the bed. She was stoic as she sank onto the mattress.

Holden pinched back the curtains, but he could not see the parking lot—only the railing of the porch that overlooked it. Turning away from the window, Holden fell against the wall.

Panic coiled over him. He pressed his eyes closed.

While Kate sat on the edge of the bed, her thoughts cleared with one focused notion: Shane was dead and Holden knew about it. She squeezed the bedspread into her fist. In a flat voice, she said,

"You knew that my brother was murdered...and yet you acted like nothing had happened."

"Kate...I—" He turned away and pressed his forehead to the wall.

"How could you?!" she shrieked.

She sprung from the bed to jump onto Holden's back. Screaming, she beat him madly about the head and shoulders with her fists.

* * * * *

Kate's screams brought everyone in the parking lot to attention. Police officers drew their automatic rifles over the hoods of their police cruisers. Galletta waved for the SWAT team to follow him, Lugowski, and Jack up the steps to the hotel room door.

Eric jumped out of the cruiser that he'd been sitting in. A police officer pushed him to the ground behind the vehicle. "Please stay down, Sir," he instructed.

* * * * *

Trying to pry Kate from his back, Holden danced around the room while she continued to scream and punch him.

"Reese!" Galletta called from the other side of the door. "Release Miss West! No one has to get hurt!"

Finally, Holden flung his body backward on top of Kate, except the gun flipped from his grip

266

and slid across the floor to land under the dresser. Rolling off of Kate's body, Holden scrambled on his hands and knees in search of his weapon.

Dazed, Kate lay on the floor with the wind knocked out of her.

"Christ almighty! Where's the fuckin' gun?" Holden rummaged over the floor.

Exhaustion overtook Kate. She closed her eyes while trying to separate herself from the situation. She had been in love with this man for almost a year. She forgave him for his infidelity with Ava. She gave up her job with Doc Spears to become his vet assistant so that they could have a future together. She loved him.

How could this be happening? At any moment, she would wake up from this nightmare. It was a bad dream—it had to have been a bad dream, because the man that she had fallen head-over-heals in love with would never murder anyone. Holden Reese was a kind, loving man. He would never hurt anyone.

Kate opened her eyes. But the nightmare continued. She rolled her head to the right. She could see the gun under the dresser.

"Reese! You've got one minute, and then we're coming in!" Galletta yelled.

Holden grabbed Kate by the arm to pull her from the floor. He shoved her onto the bed. He fell to his knees to grapple under the bed. It all seemed to be moving in slow motion as she lay on the bed like a ragdoll.

Her brother was dead. Shane was dead. He was so ornery, so cocky, so easy to set off, and so very lovable.

Now, Shane had been murdered, and she wasn't there for her father. Tears streamed down her face.

Kate took in a deep breath. The sorrow suddenly fell away replaced by an undeniable surge of rage.

Holden's betrayal flowed through her veins like a hot acid. Her eyes rotated to the Bible on the nightstand. Slowly, she stretched until she had it in her hand.

"Holden!" she yelled.

He popped his head up to look at her. With all her might and her anger, Kate slammed the Bible across his face to send him backward to the floor. Kate wasted no time. She dove to the floor onto her stomach and stretched her right arm under the dresser, but it was just beyond her reach. She stretched and pushed and wiggled until her fingers were almost to the gun, when Holden grabbed her by her leg to pull her back.

Kate clenched her left hand around the leg of the dresser. Panting, she stretched and groped along the carpeting with her fingernails for the gun. She could feel the steel at the tips of her fingers. Finally, the tip of her middle finger wrapped around the trigger.

Holden pulled and dragged her backward.

With a firm grip on the gun, she let go of the dresser's leg and let him drag her away. Holden yanked her to her feet only to face the gun at his chest. Kate was still fumbling to gain control of the gun in her grip when Holden twisted her wrist in an effort to force her to let go, but she held on!

Again, Holden found himself dancing around the room while fighting to gain control.

Somewhere in the background, from a far far away distance, they heard a man's voice yelling, "Reese! We're coming in!"

The gun wedged between their bodies exploded while the hinges ripped from the door to toss splintered wood in all directions as the SWAT team burst into the room.

~ NINETEEN ~

All guns pointed at Kate and Holden. The world stood completely still. The only thing that she could hear was the pounding of her own heart and her breathing booming inside her brain.

The SWAT team surrounded them.

She looked into Holden's eyes—they were half-lidded. Abruptly, he curled away from her and collapsed to the floor. His torso was covered in blood. So was hers. Yet, she felt no burn. No sting. She felt nothing at all.

"Drop the gun, Miss West," Galletta ordered.

Kate didn't move.

"I said drop the gun, Miss West!"

Lugowski stepped forward. He handed his gun off to Galletta. Slowly, he approached Kate. He could see that she had gone into shock. Carefully, he removed the gun from her hand and passed it off to one of the SWAT team members.

Galletta knelt down next to Holden.

"We need a medic, now!" he hollered.

Gently, Lugowski lowered Kate to the bed. She was stoic, unresponsive. Cupping her chin in his hand to turn her face toward him, Lugowski whispered, "Kate...it's okay. Everything is going to be okay. You're safe. You're with me now."

Her vacant eyes looked into his until recognition finally broke through the barrier of shock. Kate mumbled, "Carl..."

He offered her a slight smile. "Yeah, it's me, Carl."

Kate's eyes blinked. Her lips quivered, and she began to sob. Jack grabbed a blanket from the bed to wrap around her shoulders to hide the fact that she was only wearing a lacey bra on the top part of her body.

Lugowski knelt in front of her. He felt along her arms and examined her hands. He checked her tummy as it was covered in blood. "Are you hurt, sweetheart?"

"Carl..." Kate said through her weeping, "Holden's dead. I think I killed him. He said that Chip Walker killed Shane...he knew about it all along."

"Shhhh." Lugowski eased onto the bed next to her and wrapped his arms around her. She closed her eyes and pressed her face into his chest. Lugowski laid his cheek on top of her head while he stroked her hair. "Everything's okay, your brother and Dave Blake were rescued and Chip Walker is in custody."

Her face jerked away from his chest. Her eyes widened in horror. She cried, "Oh, my God! I killed him! I shot him!"

"It was self-defense, Kate," Jack said. "We saw the two of you struggling for the gun when we came through the door. It could have been either one of you lying on the floor right now."

"Don't think about it, Kate," Lugowski said. "Close your eyes, and don't think about it."

Only just then Kate could feel a weak hand tug at her jeans. She looked down to see Holden's watery eyes looking back at her.

Blood spewed from his mouth as he muttered, "I'm so sorry, Kate."

With that his head fell to the side, his beautiful brown eyes that used to mesmerize her were now vacant in death.

Kate gasped.

Lugowski enveloped her deeper into his chest as there was a sudden shift in movement about the room.

The SWAT team was vacating the area to make room for the EMTs, who examined Holden, threw a blanket over him and pronounced him dead.

Finally, Jack tapped Lugowski on the shoulder. "Lugowski, the medics are ready to examine Kate, and they're bringing Mr. West in."

Lugowski moved aside while a female EMT moved into position to examine Kate. The woman spoke softly to her and handled her with tender care. After she determined that Kate was a bit bruised and battered, she had no serious injuries. The woman wrapped a clean blanket tightly around her.

"We will be taking you to the hospital, Miss West, for routine tests and observation to make sure that everything is okay." She helped Kate from the bed and turned toward the door. Kate glanced up to see her father step into the room. Tears flooded her eyes. The paramedic stepped aside to let her rush to her father's waiting arms.

Relief washing over him, Eric swallowed her into his arms and kissed her on the top of her head. "Thank God, thank God, you're safe," he whispered into her hair.

Kate looked up at him with watery eyes. "I'm so sorry, Dad. I didn't know about Shane until a few minutes ago. I didn't know about any of it. I'm so sorry for everything."

Eric cupped her face in his hands. "It's okay, baby. Everything is fine now. Shane is fine. Dave is going to be fine, too. I'm just thankful that you're safe."

Kate blinked back. The memory of struggling with Holden for the gun and his bloodied body falling to the floor coiled through her. Her body began to shake uncontrollably. Her throat tightened. She couldn't breathe. The world was spinning all around her, and her knees began to wobble.

"Oh my God!" she wailed.

"It's okay, Kate. It's okay..." Eric reached for her, except he wasn't fast enough. Shaking her head violently while gasping for a breath, Kate collapsed to her knees while wrapping her arms around her stomach. She vomited onto the floor.

"Paramedic!" Eric called.

The woman came running toward them with Lugowski close behind. On her hands and knees, Kate dry heaved. Eric and Lugowski took her by the shoulders and helped her to her feet. The paramedic readjusted the blanket around Kate as they led her out of the motel to an ambulance.

"I killed him, Dad," she sobbed, "I killed him because I thought he had a part in Shane's murder! I thought Shane was dead!" Her words were barely intelligible through the continual hiccup of tears.

Eric strained to understand her.

Kate's face was flushed and saturated. "He was acting so nasty. It was like he was someone else—someone I didn't know, and then when he told me... he told me that Shane was dead...and that he was working with Chip...how could I forgive him for that?"

They eased her into the ambulance. The paramedic dug through her medical box before pulling a syringe and bottle out of it. She stuck the syringe into the bottle, tipped it upside down and measured a dose.

Kate wiped her face with the blanket. "I...I totally lost it! How can I ever forgive myself?"

"C'mon, sweetie, we're going to give you something to help calm you," the EMT said as she pressed a needle into Kate's arm.

Shooting the EMT an irritated look, Kate flinched. Then, just as quickly, she succumbed to the lull of oblivion that promised to be a better place than where she was at this horrid moment.

With Eric's assistance, the paramedic lowered Kate down onto the gurney inside the ambulance. Kate's eyes closed, her breathing deepened, her head fell to the side, and her body went boneless as it descended into the peaceful void.

"Is she okay?" Lugowski called from outside the ambulance.

"I hope so," Eric said.

The paramedic closed the doors, the lights flashed, and the ambulance pulled away.

Lugowski watched the ambulance roll past the police cruisers and the sea of law enforcement milling around the area until it disappeared from sight.

He let out a relieved breath. Kate was safe, and for that he was thankful. If Holden had harmed her... well, he didn't want to think about what his reaction would have been. He ran a hand over the nape of his neck and then reached into his jacket for the crinkled pack of cigarettes that he always kept on hand. He popped one into his lip, retrieved his lighter from the pocket of his slacks, and lit it. He breathed in long and deep, closing his eyes to savor the sated moment of relief.

The sound of wheels rattling along the pavement caused him to turn. They were wheeling a gurney with a black body bag marked Coroner's office past him—Holden Reese's body.

Blowing a blue miasma of smoke from his nose, Lugowski shook his head. The man had everything: a thriving veterinary practice, a beautiful woman who loved him and was going to marry him. Why the hell did he buddy-up with Chip Walker in a horse-drugging scheme? How could he think it would never be exposed? How could he throw it all away—especially when he had a woman like Kate West at his side? The woman was true blue. She was a woman any man would want to come home to every night, hold her in his arms while he slept, and wake up to those stunning eyes of hers every morning. Yep, Kate West was a keeper, and that asshole didn't appreciate it.

Lugowski dropped his chin into his chest in utter disgust. He had witnessed so many things as a homicide detective, but it was the waste that always made him shake his head, repulsed—people who had it all, and just threw it away.

"What the hell," he murmured under his breath while blowing a plume of smoke into the cool autumn morning. He watched it rise and fade away.

His cell phone vibrated in his pocket. Pulling it out, he looked at the screen: Ava West. His lips kicked up into a slight smile.

"Hey, baby..." He listened for a moment. "Yeah, she's okay." He watched as they loaded Holden's body bag into the coroner's van. "Dr. Reese didn't come out of things too well, but Kate is going to be fine...hopefully."

~ EPILOGUE ~

Two Weeks Later

The sun glimmered through the golden leaves that fluttered into Shady Deal's private paddock at Westwood Thoroughbred Farm. Perched on the fence, Kate admired the gelding wandering around the paddock and munching on the grass. Guido munched on grass right alongside the gelding. She was pleased with how well his recovery was coming. The top of the horse's head was still shaved to aid in keeping his stitches clean. The large wound that ran across his poll and down the side of his right jowl still looked ugly, but Shady Deal was well on his way to a clean bill of health.

Holden would have been pleased.

Closing her eyes, Kate shook her head. No...she wasn't going to go there.

Unfortunately, the horse would never race again.

Mike had made arrangements for a new home and a new vocation for the big gelding. He knew of a local teenage girl whose horse had died from colic earlier in the year. The girl was devastated, and her family didn't have the money to purchase a new horse due to the huge vet bill that the sick horse had incurred.

The girl was an excellent rider and very active in the local 4-H, so Mike offered up Shady Deal as a replacement—free of charge, as soon as he was totally healed.

The girl was thrilled and had been by the farm several times to visit with Shady Deal. They formed an instant bond. Moreover, the girl and her family had taken a liking to Guido who had become Shady Deal's stable companion.

Funny, Sheldon didn't seem to miss him—at all. Kate chuckled every time she thought about it.

Kate's attention was drawn to the driveway when she heard a vehicle rolling along the gravel beneath the grand oaks that were slowly allowing their leaves to patter to the ground. It wouldn't be long until old man winter would grip Pennsylvania in his wicked fist.

She recognized the white SUV when it came into view—it was Lieutenant Carl Lugowski's police vehicle. The vehicle crunched to a stop just beyond the paddock. Lugowski stepped out with a tentative smile on his face. He never displayed a wide smile, or an ear-to-ear grin, or a toothy smirk. The best he could do was svelte, and she decided that it must be his default pleasant expression.

Lugowski had beautiful eyes, yet they always seemed to be wary—much like his smile. Kate was most certain that it was because of his job. The man rarely got to see the good in people—only the wicked and most evil that they had to offer. On top of it all, in Kate's opinion, he dated a manipulative green-eyed monster: Ava.

Oftentimes, she found herself thinking that he could do so much better than that bitch. Nonetheless, the fact remained that Carl Lugowski must've found the calculating vixen enticing or he simply wouldn't be with her, right?

Lugowski strolled toward her still wearing that slight smile that flirted with the edges of his mouth. He draped his arms over the fence next to where Kate was sitting.

Nodding toward the gelding, he said, "Hey, Shady Deal is looking pretty good."

"He's going to be okay."

"What's with the goat?"

Kate snorted. "That's Guido. Punch brought him home as a stable companion for Sheldon, but since Shady Deal's incident we've been keeping the goat with him. They've become very attached. Guido will be going with Shady to his new home in a few more weeks."

"That's very good news," Lugowski said. He studied her for a moment. "How about you? Are you going to be okay?"

She looked down at him to see something different in his eyes: caring. It was sincere and warm. She favored him with a soft curl to her lips and then raised her face into the crisp breeze that lightly lifted her hair from her shoulders.

Kate said, "It's going to take some time."

"The best thing that you can do is get back to a normal routine, Kate. I hear that you're starting back with Doc Spears. That's a good thing."

Now that Holden was gone, Kate would not only be without the man she'd fallen so hard for, but she would also be among the unemployed. While her family was wealthy, Eric made sure they all were independent.

After a long discussion prompted by old Doc Spears, Ava had agreed to let Kate pick up some of the shifts at the racetrack: weekends so that Ava could be free, and, of course, the pesky emergency calls that could take up hours in the middle of the night. While it suited Ava's agenda, as most things always did, Kate accepted the gracious offer without complaint.

Lugowski glanced around the farm. It was still. "Where is everybody?"

"It's Sunday. The Steelers are playing. C'mon."

She maneuvered to hop down from her perch on the fence. Lugowski was swift to offer his hand, and she took it. When her feet made purchase with the ground, the consciousness of their entwined fingers and the closeness of their bodies brought them to a halt. The right side of Kate's mouth kicked upward. She looked at him through her lashes.

"You're hand is cold," she whispered.

"Cold hands, warm heart."

It was rather sexy. Kate chuckled. Sexy or not, she truly believed that Lugowski had a warm heart and she wondered if that cold-hearted witch that he was involved with had any appreciation for him. Kate's doubts were off the charts.

When she tried to release his hand, he tightened his grip. Surprisingly, she simply didn't mind, so hand-in-hand they strolled toward the house and climbed the stairs onto the porch where Lugowski freed her hand. She turned to look into his eyes—they were smiling at her.

When they pressed through the door into the foyer they could hear the roar of the Steeler nation bursting through the TV, along with hoots and hollers from the fans that were watching the game in the study.

"Hey! You've arrived just in time," Jen called out to them. "I believe the Steelers just scored a touchdown." They looked up to find her carrying a tray of snacks from the kitchen followed closely by Zoe with yet another tray of food. Kate was taken aback when a third person emerged from the kitchen: Taysa Quaide.

"Hey, Taysa, I didn't see your car in the drive," Kate said.

With a quick sweep of her head, Zoe flipped her dark blonde hair over her shoulder. "Punch and I brought her along." She added a wink and a spicy curl to her lips.

Kate snickered to herself. Zoe had hooked up with Punch only several months ago and she was fitting into the family like a glove. She was already taking up match-making, and it seemed that Kate's big brother, Mike, and Taysa Quaide were on her radar—big time.

You go, girl.

The study was still buzzing after the touchdown in anticipation of the field goal. When the ref's arms went up, cheers and high-fives burst through the room. Eric was the first to notice Kate and Lugowski lingering at the threshold of the study, while Jen urged the lieutenant to have one of the hot hors d'oevures from her tray.

Eric strode toward them with his hand extended. "Lieutenant, good to see you. Are you on duty?"

"No," he explained, "Jack is on assignment so I came to give Dave a lift to the airport."

Mike, Shane, Punch, and ol' Doc Spears left their seats to surround the lieutenant with hand shakes and pleasantries. Eric handed Lugowski a beer. He twisted the cap and took a hearty swig.

Dave Blake pulled up from his seat with his arm in a sling and walked toward the corner where his duffle bag waited. "Thanks for letting me stay here, Mr. West, and my parents wanted me to thank you again for the hospitality as well." He shook Eric's hand.

"Not a problem. I just wish they could've stayed longer." Eric turned to Lugowski to ask, "Where does the investigation at Keystone stand, Lieutenant?"

"Well, Chip Walker will be facing quite a bit of jail time, not only for his involvement in the drugging of the horses, but of course also for the attempted murder of your son and a police officer. There are quite a few trainers at Keystone whose names were mentioned by Chip during interrogation. They will be indicted, I'm afraid." Lugowski told them only what was appropriate.

"I don't understand how they got those scripts filled," Shane asked. "I mean, Holden was a vet, not an M.D."

"Veterinarians can write prescriptions," Doc said. "I just couldn't believe that Tony Kemp was Chip's step-brother. He seemed like such a nice guy." He let out a hearty laugh. "I thought he was gonna pee his pants when I said we were testing for everything.

Hell, I thought every trainer in the joint was gonna lose it, except for Dan, and that's when I knew he wasn't involved."

Lugowski said, "Yep, Tony would let Chip know what drugs that the track would be testing for on what dates so that Chip could make sure that the horses in his program were clean for those particular drugs. Therefore, the drugs that they used and the scripts that were being filled were on a continual rotation. It was working so well that the pharmacy wasn't filling the same kind of drugs in large quantities on a regular basis. Chip had a sweet operation: a vet to write scripts, a pharmacist to fill them, and a man in the test barn to keep him informed. Thanks to Doc Spears' vigilant watch, we were able to put an end to it. However, let's just say that Rosemount has one less pharmacist, although I'm not in the position to reveal his name." He turned to Taysa. "I suppose we owe your father an apology, Miss Quaide. He was at the top of our list of suspects, but he turned out to be clean. Sorry about that, but I'm glad it worked out."

Taysa favored him with a svelte smile. "Dad is gruff. And I can understand how he could come off as…dishonest, but he's a good man and he has adopted my herbal therapies instead of drugs to help heal the horses, Lieutenant."

Mike wrapped his arm around her waist. "Ya know, we wouldn't mind learning more about your herbal treatments, Taysa."

Her lips curled. "Really? Well, having your daddy punch my daddy in the nose isn't the best way to get on my good side," she said, looking at Eric askance. His cheeks were flushed.

Mike snorted. "We'll work on that."

Punch noticed that Kate's gaze had dropped to the floor at the mention of Holden's name. Lightly patting him on his healthy shoulder, Punch turned to Dave. "Well, I guess this means that your ridin' days are over."

Dave snorted. "Is that what I was doing? I thought I was hanging on for dear life."

"I know that's what Stan Urick thought," Shane said.

A round of laughter filled the room.

"So where does that leave you?" Mike asked. "When will you be able to go back to active duty?"

Dave shrugged with his good shoulder. "Don't know exactly. This shoulder is going to take some time to heal. It's my shooting arm, too. I think I'll be on desk duty for quite some time—if not indefinitely. I may have to rethink my career path."

Smiling, Dave took in the faces that were gathered around him. The Wests were good people. They were a tightly-knitted group who not only watched out for each other, but their fellow man, too. "Well,

I'm afraid I've got a plane to catch. Thanks again, and you all take care."

"We wish you all the best, Dave," Eric said. "Drop in on us anytime."

"I'll do that, sir."

"I'll walk you out," Kate said.

With that, Lugowski, Dave, and Kate walked toward the door while the rest of the group returned to their seats and took up their beers. There was still a quarter left in the game and the Steelers were ahead of the Browns by one touchdown and a field goal. The Browns had the ball, and the Steeler nation could be heard from the TV cheering while whipping their terrible towels over their heads.

Kate held the door open when Dave stepped onto the porch with Lugowski close behind. The sudden urge to touch him came out of nowhere, and without a thought or a hesitation, she clasped the sleeve of Lugowski's coat to bring him to a halt. "Carl..."

He turned toward her. She realized that she hadn't thought it through at all, so she offered him a thin smile. "I... I wanted to thank you for bringing Shane home safe. I don't know what we would've done had he been—"

Lugowski squeezed her hand. He looked into her eyes—even in distress her eyes made him melt. In this moment, and every moment in his heart, he was sure of one thing: Kate West was a keeper. Her hand felt warm and right in his, yet all he could think of to say was, "It makes my job so worth doing when a hostage is returned home to their family."

What? Really?

Damn, that's not what he wanted to say! He didn't want to just stand in the doorway with the autumn chill blowing through the foyer with that stupid remark hanging in the air. The truth was that he wanted to sweep her into his arms and kiss away her hurt. He wanted to tell her how beautiful she was and how her eyes mesmerized him every time he looked into them, but he'd already played the "I was just doin' my job" card.

Moron.

He swallowed hard. "You take care, pretty woman. I'll see ya around, I'm sure."

"You, too." She watched as they made their way to Lugowski's SUV. With one last wave, she closed the door.

Eric strolled into the foyer. He wrapped his arms around his daughter, and kissed her forehead.

The End? I think not!

THE DEAD OF WINTER

NOTE FROM THE AUTHOR: Thank you for reading SHADY DEALS. I hope you enjoyed the story, and I hope you will take time to read an excerpt from the next Unbridled adventure: THE DEAD OF WINTER...

Snowflakes clung to Lieutenant Carl Lugowski's eyelashes. He tucked his hands into his pockets, burying his face deeper into the upturned collar of his wool coat, hiding from January's wicked gusts bursting along the sidewalk of the Albion State Correctional Facility. His eyes hardened at the sight of the tall lanky prisoner in handcuffs who the guards led toward him.

He was several years older since Lugowski had last seen him. His face was hard-bitten from his time behind those cold cruel walls. There was still a hint of the handsome man that he used to be, except for that filthy smirk that he was wearing. Oh yeah, Bryce Masters could woo women. He could woo them right into his house of horrors to rape and torture and kill them. Twelve to be exact, over a six-year period and a four-state spread.

Lugowski locked eyes with him, remembering the mutilated bodies that Masters had left in his wake. The case had been one of his first murder investigations when he took a position in Kentucky years ago, before deciding to return to Pennsylvania. Masters had avoided the death penalty through plea bargaining. One by one he agreed to disclose the location of his victim's remains, if they would incarcerate him at Albion, rather than kill him.

Coward.

Each of the victim's parents begged the state prosecutor to make a deal with Masters. They wanted to bury their daughters with dignity, find closure, and try like hell to move forward out of the nightmare that had gripped their lives for so long. Lugowski couldn't blame the families. He understood their desperation, but he longed to see this piece of shit get the needle that he so deserved.

Masters still owed one more location of his last victim, Emily Steele. Lugowski raised his chin out from the huddle of his collar to meet him face-to-face, as the guards shoved Masters toward him. His smirk grew into a full-blown grin. Masters stood straight and proud dressed in a fine three piece suit, a fresh haircut, and a heavy wool coat draped over his squared shoulders.

At this moment Lugowski couldn't help but think of this last family. How that poor woman had suffered. Liz Steele had lost everything that she loved, her daughter and her husband, within within a short, three-week period. Mrs. Steele was now in the final stages of uterine cancer. With her own mortality quickly closing in, she was desperate to bury her daughter before time ran out. Now instead of the man responsible for so much death getting his due, he may very well be able to turn the screws again to save his worthless life. It was a hard pill for Lugowski to swallow.

"Nice suit," Lugowski grumbled, fingering the lapel with a scowl on his face.

"You know the drill. He has the right to show up at the hearing dressed like everybody else." The guard remarked.

"He's not like everybody else," Lugowski stated. His eyes locked with Masters', pitching the lapel away in disgust.

Masters liked it.

The guard's nose and cheeks were turning bright red in the icy wind and flurry. His nose began to run. He was ready to load the prisoner into Lugowski's white unmarked SUV, and return to the warmth of inside.

"Terrible day to schedule a hearing. There's a bad storm heading this way. If you need help, radio or call." He said, hoping Lugowski would soon give up the pissing contest with the prisoner and be on his way.

Lugowski's callous gaze never left Masters. "No, I want to take this one in personally. I want to see to it that he gets what's coming to him."

Masters returned Lugowski's curt smile. Lugowski whipped the back door open gesturing for him to get in. Masters slid into the backseat behind the caging resting his handcuffed wrists between his legs. Lugowski nodded to the guards, jogged around the front of the SUV, and then eddied in behind the steering wheel.

It would be a long ride, but hopefully, in the end, the last victim would be liberated from some shallow grave, in some remote location, and somehow Masters would have to pay...with his life.

**PLEASE NOTE: Changes may be made to the excerpt that you have just read during the editing process of The Dead of Winter. For more information on the Unbridled Series, the First Force Series, and all of Cindy McDonald's books, please visit her website at: www.cindymcwriter.com Hey, you can view book trailers, too!*

ABOUT CINDY MCDONALD

For twenty-six years my life whirled around a song and a dance: I was a professional dancer/choreographer for most of my adult life and never gave much thought to a writing career until 2005. Don't ask me what happened, but suddenly I felt drawn to my computer to write about things I have experienced (greatly exaggerated upon, of course) with my husband's Thoroughbreds and the happenings at the racetrack.

Surprised? Why didn't I write about my experiences with dance? Eh, believe it or not life at the racetrack is more... racy. The drama is outrageous—not that dancers don't know how to create drama, because believe me, they do, but race trackers just seem to get more down and dirty with it which makes great storytelling—great fiction.

I didn't start out writing books. The Unbridled Series started out as a TV drama, and the Hollywood readers loved the show. The problem was we just couldn't sell it. So one of the readers said to me, "Cindy, don't be stupid. Turn your scripts into a book series." And so I did!

In May of 2011 I took the big leap and exchanged my dancin' shoes for a lap top—I retired from dance. It was a scary proposition, I was terrified, but I had the full support of my husband, Saint Bill. It has been a huge change for me. I went from dancing hard five hours a night to sitting in front of a computer. I still work out and I take my dog, Harvey, for a daily run. I have to or I'd be as big as a house. Do I miss dance? Sometimes I do. I miss my students. I miss choreographing musicals, but I love my books and I love sharing them with you.

To read excerpts from future books, view book trailers, and keep up with everything that is Unbridled, please visit Cindy's website at www.cindymcwriter.com

GET TOTALLY UNBRIDLED!
CHECK OUT CINDY McDONALD'S
UNBRIDLED SERIES:

It's really quite simple. The Unbridled Series is Thoroughbred racing steeped in murder, suspense, and a generous dose of romance—hey, what more could you ask for?
Available in print or ebook at
amazon.com, BAM, barnesandnoble.com
and where all fine books are sold.

ACCOLADES FOR CINDY McDONALD'S
UNBRIDLED SERIES:

"I love this series!" ~Reviewer: Wanted Readers
"McDonald continues her dazzling writing style that keeps the reader in suspense from beginning to end." ~Reviewer: The Book Nerd
"I couldn't put it down. I finished the book in two days—something that I never do."
~Reviewer: Socrates Book Reviews.

www.cindymcwriter.com

Hey! You can view book trailers at the site as well.

Cindy loves to hear from her readers:

unbridledseries@gmail.com

CINDY McDONALD PRESENTS . . .

Into the Crossfire

The first book from her new series
FIRST FORCE

THERE'S A SCORE TO SETTLE!

It has been four years since ex Navy SEAL, Jack Haliday, had an explosive run-in with a biker gang wounding their leader, Gunner.

During those years, Jack had acquired everything he ever wanted: a beautiful wife, an adorable daughter, and a lovely home in the suburbs— everything was just about as perfect as it could get, until Gunner returned to twist Jack's world inside-out with a vengeance that he could never have prepared for.

Now Jack Haliday has a score to settle and he's got some friends to help him do it!

www.ingramcontent.com/pod-product-compliance
Lightning Source LLC
Chambersburg PA
CBHW070308260626
47160CB00003B/769